DEATH LIKES IT HOT

DEATH
LIKES IT HOT

Edgar Box

VINTAGE BOOKS
A DIVISION OF RANDOM HOUSE
NEW YORK

FIRST VINTAGE BOOKS EDITION, October 1979

Copyright 1954 by Edgar Box
All rights reserved under International and Pan-American Copy-
right Conventions. Published in the United States by Random
House, Inc., New York, and in Canada by Random House of
Canada Limited, Toronto. Originally published by E. P. Dutton
and Co., Inc., in 1954.

LIBRARY OF CONGRESS CATALOGING IN PUBLICATION DATA

Vidal, Gore, 1925-
Death likes it hot.

I. Title.
PZ3.V6668Di   1979   [PS3543.I267]   813'.5'4   79-10159
ISBN 0-394-74055-6

Manufactured in the United States of America

DEATH LIKES IT HOT

1

The death of Peaches Sandoe the midget at the hands, or rather the feet, of a maddened elephant in the sideshow of the circus at Madison Square Garden was at first thought to be an accident, the sort of tragedy you're bound to run into from time to time if you run a circus with both elephants and midgets in it. A few days later, though, there was talk of foul play.

I read with a good deal of interest the *Daily News'* account. A threatening conversation had been overheard; someone (unrevealed) had gone to the police with a startling story (unrevealed) and an accusation against an unnamed party. It was very peculiar.

Miss Flynn, my conscience and secretary, elderly, firm, intolerant, ruthless but pleasingly gray, looked over my shoulder as was her wont. "You will not, I presume . . ."

"Get involved in this grisly affair? No. Or at least not until I'm asked which is unlikely since the circus has its own public relations setup. . . ."

"It's possible that some member of the circus, how-

1

ever, knowing your propensity for Shady Personages and Crime might engage your services . . ."

"They'll have to catch me first. Miss Flynn, I'm gone." I stood up abruptly; she looked bewildered . . . wondering if perhaps I had gone over to the world of be-bops: Miss Flynn is a student of argot though her own conversation is very courtly, cool in fact.

"I'm gone for a week," I explained.

She nodded, understanding at last. "You'll accept Mrs. Veering's invitation to partake of the sun at her palatial estate on Long Island?"

"Just this moment decided. No reason to hang around here. August is a dead month. We haven't any business you can't handle better than I." She inclined her head in agreement. "So I'll go out to Easthampton and see what it is she wants me to do."

"Social Position has never been Mrs. Veering's aim." Miss Flynn is a resolute snob and follows with grim fascination Cholly Knickerbocker's rich accounts of the rich.

"Well, she won't be the first dowager we put over on an unsuspecting public."

Miss Flynn scowled. Next to my affinity for Shady Personages and Crime she dislikes nearly all the clients of my public relations firm: ambitious well-heeled characters trying to exploit products or themselves in the press. With the exception of a singing dog who lost her voice, my record has been pretty good in this crooked profession. Recently business had slowed down. In August New York dies and everybody tries to get out of the heat. Mrs. Veering's mysterious summons had come at exactly the right time.

"Alma Edderdale, I know, is a friend of yours . . . and a dear one of mine . . . it was at the advice of a friend of hers that I got your name. I do wish you could come see me here Friday to spend the week end and talk over with me a little project close to my heart. Let me know soon. Trusting you won't let me down, I am, sincerely yours, Rose Clayton Veering." That was the message on thick expensive note paper with the

2

discreet legend at the top: "The North Dunes, East-hampton, Long Island, N.Y." No hint of what she wanted. My first impulse had been to write and tell her that I'd have to have a clear idea before I came of what she wanted. But the heat of August relaxed my professionalism. A week end in Easthampton, in a big house. . . .

I dictated an acceptance telegram to Miss Flynn who snorted from time to time but otherwise said nothing.

I then fired a number of instructions in my best business-executive voice, knowing that in my absence Miss Flynn would do exactly as she pleased anyway, then we gravely shook hands and I left the office: two small rooms with two desks and a filing cabinet in East 55th Street (good address, small office, high rent) and headed down Park Avenue through the sullen heat to my apartment on 49th Street (big rooms, bad address, low rent).

2

The Long Island Cannon Ball Express pulled away from the station and there was every indication that it would be able to make Montauk before nightfall; if not . . . well, those who travel that railroad are living dangerously and they know it. Cinders blew in my face from an open window. The seat sharply cut off the circulation in my legs. The hot sun shone brazenly in my face . . . it was like the days of my childhood fifteen years (well, maybe twenty years) before, when I used to visit relatives in Southampton. Everything had changed since then except the Long Island Railroad and the Atlantic Ocean.

The *Journal American* was full of the Peaches Sandoe murder case even though there were no facts out of which to make a story. This doesn't bother newspapers, however, and there were some fine pictures of naked girls wearing sequins and plumes. Peaches Sandoe herself was, in life, a rather dowdy-looking, middle-aged midget with a 1920's bob.

I was well into the *N.Y. Globe*'s account, written by my old friend and rival Elmer Bush, when a fragrant thigh struck mine and a soft female voice said, "Excuse . . . why if it isn't Peter Sargeant!"

"Liz Bessemer!" We stared at one another in amazement though why either should have been particularly surprised I don't know since we see each other at least once a month at one party or another and I have, on several occasions, tried to get a date out of her without success since I'm shy and she is usually engaged to some young blade around town. Though it was perfectly logical that we both find ourselves on a Friday heading for a week end on Long Island by Cannon Ball Express, we professed amazement at seeing each other.

Amazement turned to excitement, at least on my part, when I found she was visiting an aunt and uncle in Easthampton. "I just had to get out of the city and since Mummy is out in Las Vegas getting a divorce" (Liz though a big girl of twenty-five with blue eyes and dark brown hair and a figure shaped like a Maiden-Form Bra ad still refers to her progenitress as "Mummy" which is significant, I think), "and I wasn't invited any place this week end, I just thought I'd go on out and stay with my aunt who's been after me all summer to visit her. So you're going to be there too?"

I nodded and we kicked the ball around a bit. She knew of Mrs. Veering, even knew her place which, it seemed, was about half a mile down the road from where *she* would be staying. I experienced lust, mild but persistent. Mentally, I caressed the generous arm of coincidence.

"I hope you're not a friend of Mrs. Veering's . . . I mean, she's perfectly nice but, well, you know. . . ."

"Kind of on the make?"

"That's putting it gently." Liz made a face; I noticed she was wearing nothing under her simple worth-its-weight-in-gold cotton dress; absolutely nothing, at least

4

from the waist up. I felt very good about this for some reason and decided Christian Dior was a regular fellow after all.

"Well, it's only a job," I said vaguely, as we rattled desperately through Jamaica. "She's got some project or other she wants me to look into for her. So, what the hell . . . it's a living and I get out of town for the week end . . . maybe longer," I added softly but Liz, according to legend at least, is the least romantic girl in New York and though she's gone around with some sharp boys in her time and no doubt given them a certain satisfaction, she has never been the type to hold hands in the moonlight or exchange radiant myopic glances across crowded rooms. She's very matter-of-fact which I like, in spite of the "Mummy" business.

"That's right." She looked at me coolly, at least as coolly as it's possible to look with the cinders flying about your head and the heat one hundred degrees Fahrenheit in the car. "You have your own firm, don't you?"

I nodded. "Ever since I left the *Globe*."

"It must be awfully interesting," she said in the vague tone of Bryn Mawr. "I'm at *Harper's Bazaar* now."

I said I didn't know she worked.

"Oh yes . . . every now and then."

"What do you do there?"

"Oh . . . well, you know: that sort of thing."

I knew indeed. All New York is the richer for these vague elegant girls with some money, a set of Tecla pearls and a number of basic black dresses who while marking time between college and their first marriage work for the fashion magazines. They are charming and they love art like nobody's business . . . zooming around the galleries on 57th Street to look at pictures and around Second Avenue to various "fun-apartments" where High Bohemia gives cocktail parties for Edith Sitwell and worries about Marlon Brando.

Liz was a member in good standing of this community but she was also careful not to get typed: she was not one of the fashionable *ugly* girls who end up mak-

5

ing a career out of that kind of thing; she kept the lines of communication open with the young Wall Street set, the Newport gang, the Palm Beach crew and even the night-club bachelors who think that 57th Street is just something you pass on your way from the Plaza to the St. Regis.

We talked about mutual acquaintances. I haven't the time to circulate much in her world but I know it well enough since it's made up of old school friends of mine as well as those professional zombies that you're bound to meet sooner or later if you live in New York and go out at all.

It wasn't until we had stopped for water, or whatever it is the train stops for besides passengers at Speonk, that I asked her what she knew about Mrs. Veering.

"I don't think I know anything about her except what everybody does. You see her around, that's all. She comes from somewhere out West and she has a lot of money from a husband who's dead, I guess. I suppose she's out to make the grade as a dowager."

This was as much as *I* knew about my hostess-to-be, so we talked of other things, agreeing to meet Saturday night at the Ladyrock Yacht Club where a big dance was being held. It was assumed I'd come as a guest of Mrs. Veering but just in case she didn't go I said I'd sneak over somehow. Liz thought this was a fine idea.

Then we read our tabloids while the train passed millions of white ducks and potatoes, the principal crop of this green island. Shortly before we arrived at East-hampton, we both agreed that someone had undoubtedly pushed Peaches Sandoe in the way of that elephant. But who?

3

The North Dunes is a large gray-clapboard house sitting high on a dune to the north of the Ladyrock Yacht Club which, in turn, is north of the village.

6

I was met by a slovenly fellow in a chauffeur's hat and overalls who spotted me right off and said Mrs. Veering had sent him to fetch me. I climbed in the station wagon which was parked with all the others beside the railroad, waved to Liz who was getting into a similar station wagon and sat back as I was driven in silence through the handsome village with its huge elm trees and silver pond and the house where somebody did not write *Home Sweet Home* but was perhaps thinking about it when he did write the song.

On the ocean front, one vast gloomy house after another sat among the treeless dunes where clumps of sword grass waved, dark upon the white sand. The lush green-gold course of the Maidstone provided a neat, well-ordered touch to the road which runs north of the village toward Montauk Point, a road off which, to left and right at this point, are the big houses and the cottages of the summer residents.

The North Dunes was one of the largest and gloomiest. A screened-in porch ran halfway around the house on the ocean side and, from the outside, the place looked like nothing so much as a palace of bleached driftwood.

Inside it was better.

A lean butler took my suitcase and showed me into the sunroom: a big chintzy place on the south side of the house with a fine view of the golf course and ocean: high trees screened the village from view.

Mrs. Veering greeted me, rising from the chair where she'd been seated beside the empty fireplace.

"I couldn't be more delighted, Mr. Sargeant, to have you here on such short notice." She shook my hand warmly: she was a big competent woman with a mass of blue hair and a pale skin from which two small blue eyes stared at the world expressionlessly. She was in her fifties with a bosom like a sandbag and a clear voice which was neither Western nor Colony-Restaurant-New-York but something in between. "Come sit over here and have a little drink. I'll ring for . . . unless you'd rather mix your own . . . it's over there. I'll just have a dash of Dubonnet: I never have anything else; just a bit before dinner is nice, don't you think?"

She gabbled away and I made all the expected answers as I mixed myself a Scotch and soda and poured her some Dubonnet over ice. Then I sat down in the fat chair opposite her and waited.

Mrs. Veering was in no hurry to get to the point.

"Alma Edderdale is coming next week, Monday, did you know that? I love her. She's staying at the Sea Spray . . . she's an old friend of yours, isn't she, yes? I'll want to see her of course. I would've asked her here but she likes to be alone and besides I have a house full of friends this week end." She finished the Dubonnet in one lightning gulp. "Friends and acquaintances," she added vaguely, looking out the window at the golf course, golden in the afternoon sun.

"I wonder . . ." I began, wanting to get to business right away.

"Will I have another? Yes, I think I might. It does me good the doctor says: 'just a touch of Dubonnet, Rose, before dinner, to warm the blood.' "

I poured a highball glass of the stuff which should, I thought, be enough to bring her blood to a boil. Two lady-like sips got her to the bottom of the glass and I could see what one of her problems undoubtedly was. Anyway, the drink seemed to do her good and her eyes glistened as she put the glass down and said, "I like a mixture, don't you?"

"A mixture of what, Mrs. Veering?" I had a feeling we were operating on two different frequencies.

"People. What else?" She smiled a dazzling smile, her dentures brilliant and expensive. "Now this week end I've tried to bring together *interesting* people . . . not just social . . . though they all are of course. Brexton is here." She paused, letting this sink in.

I was reasonably impressed . . . or maybe surprised is the better word. My interest in modern painting ranges somewhere between zero and minus ten; nevertheless, having batted around New York in pretentious circles, I've picked up a smattering and I can tell

8

Motherwell from Stuempfig with a canny eye. Brexton is one of the current heroes of 57th Street. He's in all the museums. Every year *Life* magazine devotedly takes its readers on a tour of his studio, receiving for their pains a ton of mail saying they ought to know better than waste space on a guy whose pictures aren't any better than the stuff little Sue painted last year in fourth grade. But Brexton has hit the big-time professionally and it was something of a surprise to hear that he was staying with Mrs. Veering. I found out why.

"His wife is my niece Mildred," she said, licking the ice daintily for one last drop of Dubonnet. "What a fuss there was in the family when she married him ten years ago! I mean how could we know he was going to be famous?"

I allowed this was always a hazard.

"Anyway it's terribly nice having them here. He isn't at all tiresome, though I must say I love art and artists and I don't really expect them to be like other people. I mean they *are* different, aren't they? Not gross clay like ourselves."

Speak for yourself, hon, I said to myself while I nodded brightly. I wondered if the Brextons had anything to do with my being asked for the week end: a big stunt of some kind to put him over maybe? I held my fire.

Mrs. Veering helped herself to another tumbler of Dubonnet. I noticed with admiration that her hand was steady. She chattered the whole time. "Then the Claypoles are here. They're great fun ... Newport, you know." She socked that one home; then she went back to her chair. "Brother and sister *and* utterly devoted which is so rare. They've never married, either of them, though of course both are in great demand."

This sounded like one for Dr. Kinsey or maybe Dr. Freud but I listened while Mrs. Veering told me what a nice couple they made and how they traveled together and were patrons of the arts together. I had heard of them dimly but I had no idea how old they were or what arts they patronized. Mrs. Veering assumed I knew everyone she did so she didn't bother to fill me in on them ... not that it made too much difference. I was assuming my duties would have nothing to do with this collection of guests.

She was just about to tell me all about the last guest: Mary Western Lung, the penwoman, when the butler crossed the room silently, swiftly, without warning and whispered something in her ear. She nodded then she motioned for him to leave, without instructions.

Whatever he had said to her had the effect of turning off the babble, to my relief. She was suddenly all business, in spite of the faintly alcoholic flush which burned now behind her white make-up.

"I'll come to the point, Mr. Sargeant. I need help. As to the main reason for my asking you here, I'll give you the general details right now. I plan to give a Labor Day party which I want to be the sensation of the Hamptons. It can't be cheap; it can't be obvious. I don't want anyone to know I've hired a press agent ... assuming you will take the job. I'll expect full coverage, though, in the press."

"My fee ..." I began; even as a boy scout of eleven I'd discovered that it's best to get that part of the business over first.

"Will be met." She was just as businesslike. "Write me a letter tonight saying how much you want, putting yourself on record, and I'll give you what you need." I was filled with admiration for the next few remarks which had to do with hiring me and also with her purpose.

"The reason I've picked you is because it's possible for me to have you here as a guest without people asking questions." I was duly flattered and wished I'd worn my Brooks Brothers gabardine suit. "So don't say anything about your profession; just pretend you're a ... writer." She finished brightly enough.

"I'll do my best."

"Tomorrow I'll go over the guest list with you. I think it's in good shape but you might be able to advise me. Then we'll discuss what publicity would be wisest. I shall want a very great deal."

I stopped myself just in time from asking why. That's one question in my somewhat crooked business you never ask. Being a publicist is a little like being a lawyer: you take on a case without worrying too much about anything except putting it over. I figured Mrs. Veering would let me in on her game sooner or later. If not, considering the fee I was going to ask, it didn't make a bit of difference.

"Now you'll probably want to go to your room. We dine at eight thirty." She paused; then: "I must ask a favor of you."

"What's that, Mrs. Veering?"

"Don't be disturbed by anything you might see or hear while you're in this house . . . and be discreet." Her rather silly face had grown solemn and pale while she spoke; I was alarmed by the expression in her eyes. It was almost as if she were frightened of something. I wondered what. I wondered if she might not be a little off her rocker.

"Of course I won't say anything but . . ."

She looked about her suddenly, as though afraid of eavesdroppers. Then she gestured, "Do run along now, please." I could hear footsteps in the main hall, approaching us.

I was almost to the door of the drawing room when she said, in her usual voice, "Oh, Mr. Sargeant, may I call you Peter?"

"Sure. . . ."

"*You* must call me Rose." It was like a command. Then I went out into the hall, almost bumping into a pale youngish woman who murmured something I didn't catch. She slipped into the drawing room while I went upstairs; a maid directed me to my room.

I was uneasy to say the least. I wondered whether or not I should take my bag and head for one of the local inns, like the 1770 House. I didn't need the job that much and I did need a vacation which, under the circumstances, might not be in the cards. Mrs. Veering

11

was a peculiar woman, an alcoholic. She was also nervous, frightened . . . but of what?

Out of curiosity more than anything else I decided to stay. It was one hell of a mistake.

4

At eight o'clock I went downstairs after a long bath and a slow ceremony of dressing while studying the faintly clammy but well-furnished room (all houses on dunes anywhere beside an ocean have the same musty smell) and reading the titles of the books on the night table: Agatha Christie, Marquand, the Grand Duchess Marie . . . I have a hunch those same books were beside every guest bed in the Hamptons . . . except perhaps in Southhampton they might have Nancy Mitford and maybe something off-color. I decided I would devote myself to Mrs. Christie in lieu of Miss Liz Bessemer, whom I'd probably not be able to see until Saturday, if then.

I found the other guests all milling around in the big room which was now cheerful and full of light, the curtains drawn against the evening. Everyone was there except our hostess.

The woman I had bumped into earlier came to my rescue. She was slender, not much over thirty with a pleasant muted face and dressed in gray which made her seem somehow old-fashioned, not quite twentieth-century. "I'm Allie Claypoole," she said, smiling; we shook hands. "I think I ran into you. . . ."

"In the hall, yes. I'm Peter Sargeant."

"Come and be introduced. I don't know what Rose is up to." She steered me about the room.

On a love seat for two, but just large enough for the one of her, sat Mary Western Lung, the noted pen-woman: a fat dimpled creature with a peaches-and-cream gone faintly sour complexion and hair dyed a stunning silver blonde. The fact she was very fat made

the scarlet slacks she was wearing seem even more remarkable than they were. I counted four folds in each
leg from ankle to thigh which made it seem as though
she had four knees per leg instead of the regulation
one.

Next stop was the other side of the room where Mrs.
Brexton, a small dark-haired woman with china-blue
eyes, was examining a pile of art books. I got a brisk
nod from her.

Brexton, who was supervising the tray of whisky,
was more cordial. I recognized him from his pictures: a
small, stooped man of forty with a sandy mustache, a
freckled bald pate, heavy glasses and regular, ordinary
features, a bit like his few representational paintings.

"What can I do for you?" he asked, rattling ice
around in a martini shaker. Next to, "long time no
see," I hate, "what can I do for you," but after his
wife's chilly reception I fell in with him like a long-lost
brother.

"I'll have a martini," I said. "Can I help?"

"No, not a thing. I'll have it in just a jiffy." I noticed
how long his hands were as he manipulated the shaker:
beautiful powerful hands, unlike the rest of him which
was nondescript. The fingernails were encrusted with
paint . . . the mark of his trade.

Allie Claypoole then introduced me to her brother
who'd been in an alcove at the other end of the room,
hidden from us. He was a good deal like her, a year or
two older perhaps: a handsome fellow, casual in tweed.
"Glad to meet you, Sargeant. Just rummaging around
among the books. Rose has got some fine ones; pity
she's illiterate."

"Why don't you steal them?" Allie smiled at her
brother.

"Maybe I will." They looked at one another in that
quick secret way married people do, not at all like
brother and sister: it was faintly disagreeable.

Then, armed with martinis, we joined the penwoman
beside the fire. All of us sat down except Mrs. Brexton
who stood aloof at the far end of the room. Even with-

13

out indulging in hindsight, there was a sense of expectancy in the air that night, a gray stillness, like that hush before a summer storm.

I talked to Mary Western Lung who sat on my right in the love seat. I asked her how long she'd been in Easthampton while my eye traveled about the room, my ears alerted to other conversations. Superficially, everything was calm. The Claypooles were arguing with Brexton about painting. No one paid the slightest attention to Mrs. Brexton; her isolation officially unnoticed. Yet something was happening. I suppose I was aware of it only because of my cryptic conversation with Mrs. Veering; even so, without her warnings, I think I would have got the mood on my own.

Mary Western Lung was interminable; her voice was shrill and babyish but not loud; as a matter of fact, despite the size of her person which could've easily supported a voice like a foghorn, it was very faint for all its shrillness and I found I had to bend very close to catch her words. . . .which suited her just fine for she was flirting like a mad reckless girl.

"Except now, with Eisenhower, it's all changed." What was all changed, I wondered? Not having listened to the beginning of her remarks.

"Nothing stays the same," I said solemnly; hoping this would dovetail properly. It did.

"How clever of you!" She looked at me with faintly hyperthyroid eyes; her big baby's face as happy and smooth as another part of a baby's anatomy. "I've always said the same thing. This isn't your first visit to these parts, is it?"

I told her I'd spent a lot of childhood summers here.

"Then you're an old-timer!" This news gave her a great deal of inscrutable pleasure. She even managed to get her hand on my left knee for a quick warm squeeze which almost made me jump out of my skin; except under special circumstances, I hate being touched. Fortunately, she did not look at me when she administered her exploratory pinch, her attention addressed shyly to

14

her own scarlet knees, or at least to a spot somewhere between two of the more likely creases.

I managed, after a few fairly hysterical remarks, to get to the console where the remains of the martinis were, promising I'd bring her back one. While I poured the watery remains from the shaker into my glass, Mrs. Brexton suddenly joined me. "Make me one too," she said in a low voice.

"Oh? Why sure. You like yours dry."

"Any way." She looked at her husband who was seated with his back to us, gesticulating as he made some point. There was no expression on her face but I could feel a certain coldness emanating from her, like that chill which comes from corpses after rigor has set in.

I made a slapdash martini for her and another for Mary Western Lung. Without even a "thank you" Mrs. Brexton joined the group by the fire, talking, I noticed, to Miss Claypoole only, ignoring the two men who were still arguing.

Since there was no place else to go, I had to rejoin Miss Lung who sipped her martini with daintily pursed lips on which sparkled a few long golden hairs.

"I never like anything but gin," she said, putting the drink down almost untouched. "I can even remember when my older brothers used to make it in bathtubs!" She roared with laughter at the thought of little-old-she being old enough to remember Prohibition.

I then found out why she was a noted penwoman. "I do a column called 'Book-Chat' it's syndicated all over the United States and Canada. Oh, you've read it? Yes? Well, isn't that sweet of you to say so. I put a *great deal* of myself in it. Of course I really don't have to make a living but every bit counts these days and it's a lucky thing for me it's gone over so big, the column that is. I've done it nine years."

I troweled some more praise her way, pretending I was a fan. Actually, I was fascinated, for some reason I couldn't define, by Mrs. Brexton and, as we talked, glanced at her from time to time out of the corner of my eyes: she was talking intently to Allie Claypoole who listened to what she said, a serious, almost grim expression on her face; unfortunately their voices were too low for me to catch what they were saying. Whatever it was I did not like the downward twist to Mrs. Brexton's thin mouth, the peevish scowl on her face.

"Rose tells me you're a writer, Mr. Sargeant."

Rose picked the wrong disguise, I thought to myself irritably; I could hardly hope to fool the authoress of "Book-Chat." I stalled. I told part of the truth. "I used to be assistant drama critic on the *New York Globe* up until a few years ago when I quit . . . to write a novel."

"Oh? how exciting! Throwing everything to the wind like that! To live for your art! How I envy *and* admire you! Do let me be your first reader and critic."

I mumbled something about not being finished yet but she was off, her great bosoms heaving and rippling. "I did the same, too, years ago when I was at Radcliffe. I just left school one day and told my family I was going to become a Lady of Letters. And I did. My family were Boston . . . stuffy people, but they came around when I wrote *Little Biddy Bit* . . . you probably remember it. I believe it was considered the best child's book of the era . . . even today a brand-new generation of children thrills to it; their little letters to me are heart-warming."

Heartburning seemed to me a more apt description. Then the career of Mary Western Lung was given me at incredible length. We had got her almost down to the present, when I asked what was keeping our hostess. This stopped her for a split second; then she said. "Rose is often late." She looked uncomfortable. "But then you're a friend of hers . . . you probably know all about it."

I nodded, completely at sea. "Even so . . ."

"It's getting worse. I wish there was something we could do but I'm afraid that, short of sending her to a sanitarium, *nothing* will do much good . . . and of course since she won't even *admit* it there's really no way for those of us who are her oldest and most trea-

16

sured friends to approach her. You know what her temper is!" Miss Lung shuddered.

"I thought she seemed a little, well, disturbed this evening. She . . ."

Miss Lung's hand descended with dramatic emphasis on my left thigh where it remained some seconds like a weight of lead. "I'm afraid for her!" Her high voice grew mysterious and feeble. "She's heading for a breakdown. She now thinks someone is trying to kill her."

It was out at last and I was relieved to find that Mrs. Veering was only a mild psychotic and not, as I'd first thought, really in danger of her life. I relaxed considerably, prematurely. "Yes, she told me something like that."

"Poor Rose," Miss Lung shook her head and withdrew her hand from its somewhat sensitive resting place. "It all started a few years ago when she was not included in the New York Social Register. I suppose you weathered *that* with her like all the rest of us . . . what a time it was! It was about then that her . . ." Miss Lung looked about to make sure no one else could hear. "Her *drinking* began. I remember telling Allie Claypoole (who's also from Boston by the way) that if Rose didn't get a grip on herself she'd . . ."

But grip or no grip, our hostess appeared in a magenta dinner dress, looking handsome and steady, no worse for the gallon of Dubonnet she'd drunk before dinner.

"Come along, children!" she said, waving us all toward the dining room. I admired her steadiness. She obviously had the capacity of a camel. "I'm sorry I'm late but I got held up. We have to go in now or the cook will make a scene."

It was while I accompanied Mrs. Brexton in to dinner I noticed, when she turned to speak to her husband, that across her neck, ordinarily covered by a long bob, was an ugly purple welt extending from under the ear down the side of her neck and disappearing into the high-necked dress she was wearing. It was a

17

bruise, too, not a birthmark nor a scar ... it was a new bruise.

When she turned from her husband to speak to me, hair covered the discoloration. There was an odd look in her eyes, as though she could detect in my face what it was I'd seen, what I thought for, as she made some remark about the dance to be held the next night at the Yacht Club, her hand strayed unconsciously to her neck.

5

Dinner went well enough. Mrs. Veering was in fine form, no trace of the earlier fear which had marred our first meeting. I studied her during dinner (I sat on her left; Brexton was on her right; Allie Claypoole was on *my* left). She was animated and probably quite drunk though she didn't show it except, perhaps, in the feverish brightness of her eyes and in her conversation which made no sense at all though it sounded perfectly rational.

It was a queer crew, I decided. A hostess on the make socially in spite of her alcoholism and a big snub from the Social Register; a highbrow painter; his wife whose blood could probably etch glass, with a bruise on her neck which looked as if somebody had tried to choke her to death and then decided what the hell and left the job half done. The somebody was probably her husband whose hands looked strong enough to twist off a human head like a chicken's.

And the mysterious Claypooles, brother and sister and so in love, or something. He sat next to Mrs. Brexton at dinner and they talked together intently, ignoring the rest of the company which seemed to irritate his sister. Brexton was oblivious of everyone, a good-humored, self-centered type who saw to it that the conversation never got too far away from him or from painting.

And of course my penwoman, a massive giggling

friend to man . . . at least so she seemed underneath all
the "Book-Chat." Since her score was probably quite
low, all things considered, her predatory instincts
doubtless expressed themselves only in pats and pinch-
es at which she was pretty expert.

After dinner, a little high on white wine, we all went
back to the drawing room where a card table had been
set up.

"Of course we're seven but that doesn't mean four
can't play bridge while the others are doing something
more constructive." Mrs. Veering looked brightly
around. At first everyone said they'd rather not play
but she apparently knew what she was up to and, finally, the bridge enthusiasts (I'm not one; poker's the
only card game I ever learned) flocked to the table,
leaving Mrs. Brexton, Allie Claypoole and myself in
front of the fireplace.

It was obviously up to us to do something more constructive but I couldn't think what. There's nothing
worse than being at a formal house on a week end with
a group of people you don't know and who don't particularly appeal to you. There's always the problem of
what to talk about which, in this case, was complicated
by the sour behavior of Mrs. Brexton and the
vagueness of Alice Claypoole, neither of whom seemed
happy with the arrangements either.

"I suppose you and Fletcher will be going back to
Boston after this." Mrs. Brexton snapped this out suddenly at Allie in a tone which, if it was meant to be
pleasant, missed the mark wide. Fletcher, I gathered,
was Claypoole's first name.

"Oh yes . . . I think so. We're getting a smaller place
in Cambridge, you know."

"I don't know why you won't live in New York. It's
much more interesting. Boston is dead all year 'round."
Mrs. Brexton was animated on the subject of Boston at
least. This was the first conversation I'd heard out of
her all evening.

"We like it."

19

"I suppose *you* would." The insult in this was so clear that I could hardly believe I'd got it right.

But Allie didn't seem particularly to mind. "People are different, Mildred," she said quietly. "I don't think either of us could take New York for very long."

"Speak for yourself. Fletcher likes the city and you know it. You're the one who keeps him in Boston."

Allie flushed at this. "He's always polite," she said.

"That's not what I mean." They faced each other suddenly implacable, enemies. What was going on?

A first-rate row was beginning. "What do you mean, Mildred?"

Mrs. Brexton laughed unpleasantly. "Don't play the fool with me, Allie, I'm one person who . . ."

"Partner, I *had* no hearts!" squealed Miss Lung from the table, followed by a groan from Mr. Brexton.

"For God's sake shut up, Mildred," Allie said this under the squeal of Miss Lung but I heard her if the others didn't.

"I've shut up too long." Mrs. Brexton seemed to subside, though; her spasm of anger replaced by her usual unpleasant expression. I noticed her hands shook as she lighted a cigarette. Was she another alcoholic? One, of course, was par for any week end. Two looked like a frame-up.

Miss Claypoole turned to me as though nothing unpleasant had been said. "I'm sure you'll have something good to say about Boston," she said, smiling. "I seem to be a minority here."

I told her I'd gone to Harvard and this forged a link between us so strong that, without another word, without even a good night to her hostess, Mrs. Brexton left the room.

"Did I say anything to upset her?" I asked innocently. I was curious to know what was going on.

Allie frowned slightly. "No, I don't think so." She glanced at the bridge tables; the others were engrossed, paying no attention to us. "Mildred isn't well. She . . . well, she's just had a nervous breakdown."

So that was it. "What form did it take?"

She shrugged. "What form do they usually take? She went to bed for a month. Now she's up and around. She's really quite nice ... don't get a wrong impression of her. Unfortunately, she makes almost no sense and you can see she's as nervous as a cat. We don't quarrel with her if we can help it. She doesn't mean to be as ... as awful as she sounds."

"And she sounds pretty awful?"

"She's an old friend of mine," Allie said sharply.

"I'm sure she is," I said, not at all taken aback ... if you're among eight-balls you have to be one yourself to survive and I had two more days of this ahead of me and I didn't intend to be buffaloed at the beginning. Besides, I liked Allie. In her subdued way she was very good-looking and she had the sort of figure I like: slender and well-proportioned, no serious sags and a lovely clear skin. I imagined her without any clothes on; then quickly dressed her again in my mind: that wouldn't do at all, I decided. Besides, there was the luscious Liz Bessemer down the road waiting for me, or at least I hoped she was. One advantage of being an unmarried male in your early thirties is that most of your contemporaries are safely married and you have the field of single women to yourself, officially that is.

Allie unaware that she'd been brutally undressed and dressed again all in the space of a second, was talking about Mildred Brexton. "She's always been high-strung. That whole family is ... even Rose." She nodded toward our hostess. "I suppose you know Rose is her aunt."

I said I did.

"We met them, Fletcher and I, about fifteen years ago when Rose came East and decided to do Newport where we always go in the summers ... at least we used to. Mildred's the same age as my brother and they were, are great friends. In fact, people always thought they'd get married but then she met Brexton and of course they've been very happy." I knew she was lying: if only because it seemed unlikely any man could get along with that disagreeable woman.

21

"I suppose you've known Rose a long time." The question was abrupt.

"No, not very." I didn't know what to say, not knowing what Mrs. Veering had said.

She helped me out. "Oh, I thought Rose said you were an old friend but then she's so vague. I've seen her ask people here under the impression she's known them for years and it's turned out they're absolute strangers. That's one of the reasons her parties are so successful: everyone's treated like a long-lost cousin."

The butler slithered into the room at that moment and came, to my surprise, to me: "Mr. Sargeant, sir, you are wanted on the telephone." An honest-to-god English butler who said "telly-phone."

It was Liz. "Oh, hi, Peter. I wondered what you were doing."

"I've been wondering that myself."

"Dull?"

"Deadly. How's your place?"

"Not much better. Will you be at the dance tomorrow night?"

"I don't know. One of the guests mentioned it so I figured we'll go; if not . . ."

"Come anyway. Say you're my guest. I'll leave a note at the door for you."

"I'll like that. It's a full moon, too."

"A full what?"

"Moon."

"Oh, I thought you said 'room.' Well, I'll be looking for you."

We hung up. I felt very much better. I had visions of the two of us rolling amorously in the deserted dunes while the moon turned the sea and the sand to silver. Maybe this job wasn't going to be as grim as I thought.

Around midnight, the bridge game broke up and everybody had a nightcap except our hostess who had what could only be called an Indian war bonnet: a huge brandy glass half filled with enough cognac to float me straight out to sea.

"I hope we're not too dull for you," she said, just before we all parted for bed.

"I couldn't be having a better time," I lied.

"Tomorrow we'll do a little business and then of course we're going to the Yacht Club dance where you can see some young people."

"And what's wrong with us?" asked Miss Lung roguishly.

I was not honor-bound to answer that and after a round of good nights, we all went upstairs. I followed Mary Western Lung and the sight of those superb buttocks encased in red slacks would, I knew, haunt my dreams forever.

To my dismay, I found her room was next to mine. "What a coincidence!" was her observation.

I smiled enigmatically, ducked into my room, locked the connecting door and then, just to be safe, moved a heavy bureau against the door. Only a maddened hippopotamus could break through that barricade; as far as I knew, Miss Lung was not yet maddened.

I slept uneasily until three-thirty when, right in the middle of a mild, fairly standard nightmare (falling off a cliff), I was awakened by three sharp screams, a woman's screams.

I sat bolt upright at the second scream; the third one got me out of bed; stumbling over a chair, I opened the door and looked out into the dimly lit hall. Other heads were appearing from doorways. I spotted both Claypooles, Miss Lung and, suddenly, Mrs. Veering who appeared on the landing, in white, like Lady Macbeth.

"Do go back to sleep," she said in her usual voice. "It's nothing . . . nothing at all. A misunderstanding."

There was a bewildered murmur. The heads withdrew. I caught a glimpse of Miss Lung's intricate nightdress: pink decorated with little bows befitting the authoress of *Little Biddy Bit.* Puzzled, uneasy, I dropped off to sleep. The last thing I remember thinking was how strange it was that Mrs. Veering had made no explanation of those screams.

At breakfast there was a good deal of talk about the

23

screams ... that is at first there was until it became quite clear that one of our company had been responsible for them; at which moment everybody shut up awkwardly and finished their beef and kidney pie, an English touch of Mrs. Veering's which went over very big.

I guessed, I don't know why, that Mrs. Brexton had been responsible; yet at breakfast she seemed much as ever, a little paler than I remembered but then I was seeing her for the first time in daylight.

We had coffee on the screened-in porch which overlooked the ocean: startlingly blue this morning with a fair amount of surf. The sky was vivid with white gulls circling overhead. I amused myself by thinking it must really be a scorcher in the city.

After breakfast everybody got into their bathing suits except, fortunately, Mary Western Lung who said the sun "simply poached her skin." She got herself up in poisonous yellow slacks with harlequin dark glasses and a bandana about her head.

Mrs. Veering was the only one who didn't change. Like all people who have houses by the sea she wasn't one for sun-bathing or swimming.

"Water's too cold for me," she said, beckoning me into the alcove off the drawing room.

She was all business. I thought longingly of the beach and the surf. I could hear the sound of the others splashing about.

"I hope you weren't disturbed last night," she said, sitting down at a handsome Queen Anne desk while I lounged in an armchair.

"It was unexpected," I admitted. "What happened?"

"Poor Mildred." She sighed. "I think she has persecution-mania. It's been terrible this last year. *I* don't understand any of it. There's never been anything like it in our family, ever. Her mother, my sister, was the sanest woman that ever drew breath and her father was all right too. I suppose it's the result of marrying an artist. They *can* be a trial. They're different, you know, not like us."

24

She developed that theme a little; it was a favorite one with her. Then: "Ever since her breakdown last winter she's been positive her husband wants to kill her. A more *devoted* husband, by the way, you'll never find."

The memory of that ugly bruise crossed my mind uneasily. "Why doesn't she leave him?"

Mrs. Veering shrugged. "Where would she go? Besides, she's irrational now and I think she knows it. She apologized last night when . . . when it happened."

"What happened?"

"They had a row . . . just a married persons' quarrel, nothing serious. Then she started to scream and I went downstairs . . . their bedroom's on the first floor. She apologized immediately and so did he but, of course, by then she'd managed to wake up the whole house."

"I should think her place was in a rest home or something."

Mrs. Veering sighed. "It may come to that. I pray not. But now here's the guest list for the party. I'll want you to make a press list for me and . . ."

Our business took about an hour; she had the situation well in hand and, though I didn't dare say so, she was quite capable of being her own press agent. She had a shrewd grip on all the problems of publicity. My job, I gathered, was to be her front. It was just as well. We decided then on my fee, which was large, and she typed out an agreement between us with the speed and finesse of an old-time stenographer. "I studied typing," she said simply, noticing my awe. "It was one of the ways I used to help my late husband. I did everything for him."

We each signed our copy of the agreement and I was dismissed to frolic on the beach; the last I saw of Mrs. Veering was her moving resolutely toward the console which held, in ever-readiness, ice and whisky and glasses.

On the beach, the others were gathered.

The sun was fiercely white and the day was perfect with just enough breeze off the water to keep you cool.

I looked at my fellow house guests with interest: it's always interesting to see people you know only dressed without any clothes on, or not much that is.

Both Allie and Mrs. Brexton had good figures. Allie's especially; she looked just about the way she had the night before when I had mentally examined her ... the only flaw perhaps was that she was a little short in the legs; otherwise, she was a good-looking woman, prettier in the sun wearing a two-piece bathing suit than in her usual dull clothes. She was stretched out on a blanket next to her brother who was a solid-looking buck with a chest which had only just begun to settle around the pelvis.

Mrs. Brexton was sitting on the edge of a bright Navajo blanket in the center of which, holding a ridiculous parasol, was Miss Lung, sweating under all her clothes while Brexton, burlier than I'd thought, did handstands clumsily to show he was just as young as he felt which apparently wasn't very young.

Miss Lung hailed me. "You must sit here!" She pounded the blanket beside her.

"That's O.K." I said. "I don't want to crowd you." I sat down cross-legged on the sand between the blanket where she sat and the Claypooles. I was a good yard from her busy fingers.

"My, I've never seen such *athletic* men!" Behind her harlequin dark glasses, I could see I was being given the once-over.

At that moment Brexton fell flat on his face. Spluttering in the sand, he said, "Rock under my hand ... sharp damn thing." He pretended his hand hurt while Allie and I exchanged amused glances.

"None of us is as young as we used to be," said her brother, chuckling, pulling himself up on his elbow. "You're getting more like Picasso every day."

"Damned fraud," said the painter irritably, rubbing the sand out of his face. "Nine tenths of what he's done I could do better ... *anybody* could do better."

"And the other tenth?"

"Well, that. . . ." He shrugged. I'd already found that

26

Brexton, like most painters, hated all other living painters, especially the grand old men. He differed from
most in that he was candid, having perhaps more confidence.

He harrangued us a while in the brilliant light. I
stretched out and shut my eyes, enjoying the warmth
on my back. The others did the same, digesting breakfast.

Claypoole was the first to go in the water. Without
warning, he leaped to his feet and dashed down to the
ocean, diving flat and sharp into the first breaker. He
was a powerful swimmer and it was a pleasure to watch
him.

We all sat up. Then Mrs. Brexton walked slowly
down to the water's edge where she put on her bathing
cap, standing, I could see, in such a way as to hide
from us the long bruise on her neck.

She waded out. Brexton got to his feet and followed
her. He stopped her for a moment and they talked;
then he shrugged and she went on by him, diving awkwardly into the first wave. He stood watching her, his
back to us, as she swam slowly out toward Claypoole.

Allie turned to me suddenly. "She's going too far.
There's an awful undertow."

"She seems like a fair swimmer. Anyway your
brother's there."

"My!" exclaimed Miss Lung. "They swim like por-
poises. How I envy them!"

Claypoole was now beyond the breakers, swimming
easily with the undertow which, apparently, was pulling
south for he was already some yards below where he'd
gone into the water; he was heading diagonally for
shore.

Mrs. Brexton was not yet beyond the breakers; I
could see her white bathing cap bobbing against the
blue.

Allie and I both got to our feet and joined Brexton
at the water's edge. The water was cold as it eddied
about our ankles.

27

"I don't think Mildred should go so far out," said Allie.

Brexton nodded, his eyes still on his wife. "I told her not to. Naturally that was all she needed."

"It's quite an undertow," I said, remembering something about trajectory, about estimated speed: Claypoole was now sliding into shore on the breakers at least thirty feet below us.

As far as the eye could see to north and south the white beach, edged by grassy dunes, extended. People, little black dots were clustered in front of each house. While, a mile or two down, there was a swarm of them in front of the club.

The sky was cloudless; the sun white fire.

Then, without warning, Brexton rushed into the water. Half-running, half-swimming, he moved toward his wife.

She had made no sound but she was waving weakly on the line where the surf began. The undertow had got her.

I dived in too. Allie shouted to her brother who was already on the beach. He joined us, half-running, half-swimming out to Mildred.

Salt water in my eyes, I cut through the surf, aware of Claypoole near me. I never got to Mildred though. Instead, I found myself trying to support Brexton some feet away from his wife. He was gasping for air. "Cramp!" He shouted and began to double up, so I grabbed him while Claypoole shot beyond me to Mildred. With some difficulty, I got Brexton back to shore. Claypoole floated Mildred in.

Exhausted, chilled from the water, I rolled Brexton onto the sand. He sat there for a moment trying to get his breath, holding his side with a look of pain. I was shaking all over from cold, from tension.

Then we both went up on the terrace where the others had gathered in a circle about the white still body of Mildred Brexton.

She lay on her stomach and Claypoole squatted over her, giving artificial respiration. I noticed with horrified fascination the iridescent bubbles which had formed upon her blue lips. As he desperately worked her arms, her lungs, the bubbles one by one burst.

For what seemed like a hundred years there was no sound but that of Claypoole's exhausted breathing as he worked in grim silence. It came like a shock to us when we heard his voice, the first voice to speak. He turned to his sister, not halting in his labor, and said, "Doctor . . . quick."

The sun was at fierce noon when the doctor came, in time to pronounce Mildred Brexton dead by drowning.

Bewildered, as shaky as a defeated boxer on the ropes, Claypoole stood swaying over the dead woman, his eyes on Brexton. He said only two words, said them softly, full of hate. "You devil!" They faced each other over the dead woman's body. There was nothing any of us could do.

Chapter Two

1

Shortly before lunch, to everyone's surprise, a policeman in plain clothes arrived. "Somebody sent for me,"
he announced gloomily. "Said somebody drowned." He
was plainly bored. This kind of drowning apparently
was a common occurrence in these parts.

"I can't think who sent for you," said Mrs. Veering
quickly. "We have already notified the doctor, the fu-
neral home. . . ."

"*I* called the police," said Claypoole. Everyone
looked at him, startled. But he didn't elaborate. We
were all seated about the drawing room . . . all of us
except Brexton who had gone to his room after the
drowning and stayed there.

The policeman was curt, wanting no nonsense. "How
many you ladiesgemmen witness the accident?"

Those who had said so. Mrs. Veering, a tankard of
Dubonnet in one hand and a handkerchief in the other,
began to explain how she'd been in the house but if
she'd only known that poor Mildred . . .

The policeman gave her one irritable look and she

31

subsided. Her eyes were puffy and red, and she seemed really upset by what had happened. The rest of us were surprisingly cool. Death when it strikes so swiftly, unexpectedly, has an inexplicable rightness about it, like thunder or rain. Later grief, shock, remorse set in. For now we were all a little embarrassed that we weren't more distressed by the drowning of Mildred Brexton before our eyes.

"O.K." The policeman took out a notebook and a stub of pencil. "Give me names real slow and age and place of birth and occupation and relation to deceased and anything you remember about the incident."

There was an uneasy squeak from Mary Western Lung. "I can't see what our occupations and . . . and ages have to do with . . ."

The policeman sighed. "I take all you one by one and what you tell me is in strict confidence." He glanced at the alcove off the drawing room.

Mrs. Veering said, "By all means. You must interview us singly and I shall do everything in my power to . . ."

The policeman gestured to Miss Lung to follow him and they crossed the room together, disappearing into the alcove.

The rest of us began to talk uncomfortably. I turned to Allie Claypoole who sat, pale and tense, beside me on the couch. "I didn't know it could happen like that . . . so fast," I said, inadequately.

She looked at me for one dazed moment; then, with an effort, brought me into focus. "Do give me a cigarette."

I gave her one; I lit it for her; her hands trembled so that I was afraid I might burn her. One long exhalation, however, relaxed her considerably. "It was that awful undertow. I never go out that far. I don't know why Mildred did . . . except that she is . . . she *was* a wonderful swimmer."

I was surprised, recalling the slow awkward strokes. "I thought she looked sort of weak . . . swimming, that is."

Across the room Mrs. Veering was crying softly into her Dubonnet while Fletcher Claypoole, calm now, his mysterious outburst still unexplained, tried to comfort her. From the alcove I heard a high shrill laugh from Mary Western Lung and I could almost see that greedy fat hand of hers descending in a lustful arc on the policeman's chaste knee.

"I suppose it was her illness," said Allie at last. "There's no other explanation. I'm afraid I didn't notice her go in. I wasn't aware of anything until Brexton started in after her."

"Do you think a nervous breakdown could affect the way somebody swam? Isn't swimming like riding a bicycle, you do it or you don't?"

"What are you suggesting?" Her eyes, violet and lovely, were turned suddenly on mine.

"I don't know." I wondered why she was suddenly so sharp. "I only thought . . ."

"She was weakened, that's all. She'd been through a great deal mentally and apparently it affected her physically. That's all."

"She might've had what they call the 'death wish.' "

"I doubt if Mildred wanted to die," said Allie, a little drily. "She wasn't the suicide-type . . . if there is such a thing."

"Well, it can be unconscious, can't it?" Like everyone else I am an expert in psychoanalysis: I can tell a trauma from a vitrine at twenty paces and I know all about Freud without ever having read a line he's written.

"I haven't any idea. Poor Brexton. I wonder what he'll do now."

"Was it that happy a marriage?" I was surprised, remembering the bruise on her neck, the screams the night before: happy didn't seem the right word for whatever it was their life had been together.

Allie shrugged. "I don't think there are any very happy marriages, at least in our world, but there are people who quarrel a lot and still can't live without each other."

33

"They were like that?"

"Very much so ... especially when she began to crack up ... he was wonderful with her, considering the fact he's got a terrible temper and thinks of no one but himself. He put up with things from her that ... well, that you wouldn't believe if I told you. He was very patient."

"Was she always this way? I mean the way she seemed last night?"

Allie didn't answer immediately. Then she said, "Mildred was what people call difficult most of her life. She could charm anybody if she wanted to; if she didn't want to, she could be very disagreeable."

"And at the end she didn't want to?"

"That's about it."

Mary Western Lung in high good humor emerged, giggling from the alcove. The policeman, red of face and clearly angry, said: "You next," nodding at Allie. Miss Lung took her place beside me.

"Oh, they're so wonderful these police people! It's the first time I've ever talked to one that close and under such grim circumstances. He was simply wonderful with me and we had the nicest chat. I love the virile he-man type, don't you?"

I indicated that I could take he-men or leave them alone.

"But of course you're a man and wouldn't see what a woman sees in them." I resented faintly not being included among that rugged number; actually, our police friend could have been wrapped around the smallest finger of any athlete; however, Miss Lung saw only the glamor of the job ... the subhuman gutturals of this employee of the local administration excited the authoress of "Book-Chat." She scrounged her great soft pillow of flank against mine and I was pinned between her and the arm of the couch.

I struck a serious note in self-defense. "Did he have anything interesting to say about the accident?"

The penwoman shook her head. I wondered wildly if there was a bone beneath that mass of fat which flowed like a Dali soft watch over my own thigh; she was more like a pulpy vegetable than a human being, a giant squash. "No, we talked mostly about books. He likes Mickey Spillane." She wrinkled her nose which altered her whole soft face in a most surprising way; I was relieved when she unwrinkled it. "I told him I'd send him a copy of *Little Biddy Bit* for his children but it seems he isn't married. So I told him he'd love reading it himself . . . so many adults do. I get letters all the time saying . . ."

I was called next but not before I had heard yet another installment in the life of Mary Western Lung.

The policeman was trying to do his job as quickly as possible. He sat scribbling in his notebook; he didn't look up as I sat down in the chair beside the Queen Anne desk.

"Name?"

"Peter Cutler Sargeant Two."

"Two what?" He looked up.

"Two of the same name, I guess . . . the second. You make two vertical lines side by side."

He looked at me with real disgust.

"Age . . . place of birth . . . present address."

"Thirty-one . . . Hartford, Connecticut . . . 280 East 49th Street."

"Occupation?"

I paused, remembering my promise to Mrs. Veering. I figured, however, the law was reasonably discreet. "Public relations. My own firm. Sargeant Incorporated: 60 East 55th Street."

"How long know deceased?"

"About eighteen hours."

"That's all." I started to go; the policeman stopped me, remembering he'd forgotten an important question. "Notice anything unusual at time of accident?"

I said I hadn't.

"Describe what happened in own words." I did exactly that, briefly; then I was dismissed. Now that I look back on it, it seems strange that no one, including myself, considered murder as a possibility.

2

Lunch was a subdued affair. Mrs. Veering had recovered from her first grief at the loss of a beloved niece and seemed in perfect control of herself or at least perfectly controlled by the alcohol she'd drunk which, in her case, was the same thing.

Brexton received a tray in his own room. The rest of us sat about awkwardly after lunch making conversation, trying not to mention what had happened and yet unable to think of anything else to talk about.

The second reaction had begun to set in and we were all shocked at last by what had happened, especially when Mrs. Veering found Mildred's scarf casually draped over the back of a chair, as though she were about to come back at any moment and claim it.

It had been originally planned that we go to the Maidstone Club for cocktails but at the last minute Mrs. Veering had canceled our engagement. The dance that night was still in doubt. I had made up my mind, however, that I'd go whether the others did or not. I hoped they wouldn't as a matter of fact: I could operate better with Liz if I were on my own.

I had a chat with Mrs. Veering in the alcove while the others drifted about, going to their rooms, to the beach outside . . . in the house, out of the house, not quite knowing, any of them, how to behave under the circumstances. No one wanted to go in the water, including myself. The murderous ocean gleamed blue and bright in the afternoon.

"Well, do you think it will upset things?" Mrs. Veering looked at me shrewdly.

"Upset what?"

"The party . . . what else? This will mean publicity for me . . . the wrong kind."

I began to get her point. "We have a saying . . ."

"All publicity is good publicity." She snapped that

36

out fast enough. "Socially, however, that isn't true. Get a certain kind of publicity and people will drop you flat."

"I can't see how having a guest drown accidentally should affect you one way or the other."

"If that's all there is to it, it won't." She paused significantly; I waited for more of the same but she shifted her line of attack. "When the newspaper people come, I want you to act as my spokesman. One is on his way over here right now. But don't let on what your job really is. Just say you're a guest and that I'm upset by what's happened . . . as indeed I am . . . and that you've been authorized to speak for me."

"What'll I say?"

"Nothing." She smiled. "What else can you say? That Mildred was my niece; that I was very fond of her; that she'd been ill (I think you'd better make some point of that) and her strength wasn't equal to the undertow."

"They've taken it . . . her, the body I mean, to the morgue, haven't they?" The doctor and Brexton had carried her in to the house and I hadn't seen the corpse again.

"I don't know. The doctor took it away in an ambulance. I've already made arrangements for the undertakers to look after everything . . . they're in touch with the doctor who is an old friend of mine." She paused thoughtfully, fiddling with the pile of papers on her desk. I was surprised by the rapid change in her mood. I attributed this to her peculiar habits. Most alcoholics I knew were the same: gregarious, kindly, emotional people, quite irresponsible in every way and unpredictable. I had sat next to her at lunch and what had seemed to be a tumbler full of ice water was, I'd noticed on closer examinaion, a glass full of gin. At the end of lunch the glass was empty.

Then she said: "I would appreciate it, Peter, if nothing were said about the . . . the misunderstanding last night."

"You mean the screams?"

37

She nodded. "It could do me a great deal of harm socially if people were to get ... well, the wrong idea about Brexton and Mildred. He was devoted to her and stayed at her side all through that terrible breakdown. I don't want there to be any misunderstandings about that."

"Are there apt to be any? The poor woman went swimming and drowned; we all saw it happen and that's that."

"I know. Even so, you know what gossips people are. I shouldn't like one of the newspapermen, one of those awful columnists, to start suggesting things."

"I'll see to it," I said with more authority than was strictly accurate under the circumstances.

"That's why I want you to handle the press for me ... and another thing," she paused; then: "Keep the others away from the newspapermen."

I was startled by this request. "Why? I mean what difference does it make? We all saw the same thing. The police have our testimonies."

"The police will keep their own counsel. Just do as I ask and I'll be very grateful to you."

I shrugged. "If I can, I will, but what's to stop one of your guests from talking to the press?"

"You, I hope." She changed the subject. "I've had the nicest chat with Alma Edderdale who wishes to be remembered to you. She checked in at the Sea Spray this morning."

"That's nice."

"I'd hoped to have her over tomorrow but since this ... well, I don't quite know how to act."

"As usual, I'd say. It's a terrible tragedy but ..."

"But she was my niece and very close to me ... it wasn't as if she were, well, only a guest." I realized that I was expendable. "Perhaps we can just have a few people over ... friends of the family. I'm sure that'd be proper."

"I have an invitation," I said boldly, "to go to the Yacht Club dance tonight and I wondered, if you weren't going, whether I might ..."

38

"Why certainly, go by all means. But please, please don't talk to anyone about what has happened. I can't possibly go and I'm not sure the others would want to either since they were all more or less connected with Mildred. You of course have no reason not to." And, feeling like a servant being given Thursday afternoon off, I was dismissed while Mrs. Veering took off for her bedroom and, no doubt, a jug of the stuff which banishes care.

An hour later, I had the drawing room all to myself, which was fortunate because the butler advanced upon me with a member of the press, a chinless youth from one of the News-Services.

I waved him into a chair grandly.

"I want to speak with Mrs. Rose Clayton Veering and Mr. Paul Brexton," said the newshawk firmly, adenoidally.

"You must be satisfied with me."

"I came here to talk with Mrs. Rose . . ."

"And now you must talk to me," I said more sharply. "I am authorized to speak for Mrs. Veering."

"Who are you?"

"Peter Cutler Sargeant II."

He wrote this down slowly in what he pretended was shorthand but actually was I could see, a sloppy form of longhand. "I'd still like to . . ." he began stubbornly, but I interrupted him.

"They don't want to talk, Junior. You talk to me or get yourself out of here."

This impressed him. "Well, sir, I've been to see the police and they say Mrs. Brexton was drowned this morning at eleven six. That right?"

I said it was. I fired all the facts there were at him and he recorded them.

"I'd like to get a human interest angle," he said in the tone of one who has just graduated from a school of journalism, with low marks.

"You got plenty. Brexton's a famous painter. Mrs. Veering's a social leader. Just rummage through your

39

morgue and you'll find enough stuff to pad out a good feature."

He looked at me suspiciously. "You're not working for any paper, are you?"

I shook my head, "I saw a movie of *The Front Page* once . . . I know all about you fellows."

He looked at me with real dislike. "I'd like to see Mrs. Veering just to . . ."

"Mrs. Veering is quote prostrate with grief unquote. Paul Brexton quote world-famous modern painter refuses to make any comment holding himself incommunicado in his room unquote. There's your story."

"You're not being much help."

"It's more help than nothing. If I didn't talk nobody would." I glanced anxiously around to make sure none of the other guests was apt to come strolling in. Fortunately, they were all out of sight.

"They're doing an autopsy on Mrs. Brexton and I wondered if . . ."

"An autopsy?" This was unusual.

"That's right. It's going on now. I just wondered if there was any hint . . ."

"Of foul play? No, there wasn't. We all witnessed her death. Nobody drowned her. Nobody made her swim out into the undertow. She'd had a nervous breakdown recently and there's no doubt but that had something to do with her death."

He brightened at this: I could almost read the headline: "Despondent Socialite Swims to Death at Easthampton." Well, I was following orders.

I finally got him out of the house and I told the butler, in Mrs. Veering's name, to send any other newspaper people to me first. He seemed to understand perfectly.

Idly, wondering what to do next, I strolled out onto the porch and sat down in a big wicker armchair overlooking the sea. Walking alone beside the water was Allie Claypoole. She was frowning and picking up shells and stones and bits of seaweed and throwing them out onto the waves, like offerings. She was a lovely figure, silhouetted against the blue.

I picked up a copy of *Time* magazine to learn what new triumphs had been performed by "the team" in Washington. I was halfway through an account of the President's golf scores in the last month at Burning Tree when I heard voices from behind me.

I looked about and saw they were coming from a window a few feet to my left. The window, apparently, of Brexton's bedroom: it was, I recalled, the only downstairs bedroom. Two men were talking. Brexton and Claypoole. I recognized their voices immediately.

"You made her do it. You knew she wasn't strong enough." It was Claypoole: tense, accusing.

Brexton's voice sounded tired and distant. I listened eagerly; the magazine slipped from my lap to the floor while I strained to hear. "Oh, shut up, Fletcher. You don't know what you're saying. You don't know anything about it."

"I know what she told me. She said . . ."

"Fletcher, she was damned near out of her mind these last few months and you know it as well as I do . . . better, because you're partly to blame."

"What do you mean by that crack?"

"Just what I say. Especially after Bermuda." There was a long pause. I wondered if perhaps they had left the room.

Then Claypoole spoke, slowly: "Think whatever you want to think. She wasn't happy with you, ever. You and your damned ego nearly ruined her . . . did ruin her."

"Well, I don't think you'll be able to blame her death on my ego. . . ."

"No, because I'm going to blame it on you."

A cold shiver went down my spine. Brexton's voice was hard. "There's such a thing as criminal libel. Watch out."

"I expect to. I'm going to tell the whole story in court. I expect you thought I'd be too afraid of repercussions . . . well, I'm not. When I get through there won't be anybody who doesn't know."

Brexton laughed shortly. "In court? What makes you think there'll be a court?"

"Because I'm going to tell them you murdered her."

"You're out of your mind, Fletcher. You were there. How could I murder her? Even if I wanted to?"

"I think I know. Anyway it'll be your word against mine as to what happened out there, when she was drowning."

"You forget that young fellow was there too. You've got his testimony to think about. He knows nothing funny happened."

"I was closer. I saw . . ."

"Nothing at all. Now get out of here."

"I warned you."

"Let me warn you then, Fletcher: if you circulate any of your wild stories, if you pin this . . . this accident on me, I'll drag Allie into the case."

Before I could hear anything more, the butler appeared with the news that a reporter from the local paper was waiting to see me. Cursing my bad luck, puzzled and appalled by what I had heard, I went into the drawing room and delivered my spiel on the accidental death of Mildred Brexton. Only I wasn't too sure of the accident part by this time.

3

For some reason, the newspapers scented a scandal even before the police or the rest of us did. I suppose it was the combination of Mrs. Veering "Hostess" and Paul Brexton "Painter" that made the story smell like news way off.

I spent the rest of that afternoon handling telephone calls and interviewers. Mrs. Veering kept out of sight. Mary Western Lung proved to be a source of continual trouble, however, giving a series of eyewitness accounts of what had happened calculated to confuse an electric eye much less a bewildered newspaperman.

"And so you see," she ended breathlessly to the local newspaperman who sat watching her with round frightened eyes, "in the midst of life we are we know not where, ever. I comprehend full well now the meaning of that poor child's last words to me, I hope the water isn't cold. *Think* what a world of meaning there was in that remark now that we know what she intended to do."

"Are you suggesting Mrs. Brexton killed herself?" The member of the fourth estate was drooling with excitement.

I intervened quickly, pushing him to the door. "Of course not," I said rapidly. "There's no evidence at all that she wanted to do such a thing; as a matter of fact, she couldn't've been more cheerful this morning. . . ."

"And I'll send you a copy of 'Book-Chat,' the last one." Miss Lung shouted at the retiring interviewer's back. I told the butler to let no one else in for the day.

I turned to Miss Lung. "You know that Mrs. Veering asked me to look after the press, to keep them from doing anything sensational. Now you've gone and put it in their heads that she intended to commit suicide."

"*Did* commit suicide." Miss Lung smiled wisely at me over her necklace of chins.

"How do you know?"

"She was a marvelous athlete . . . a perfect swimmer. She deliberately drowned."

"In full view of all of us? Like that? Struggling? Why, I saw her wave for help."

Miss Lung shrugged. "She may have changed her mind at the last minute . . . anyway you can't tell me she would've drowned like that if she hadn't wanted to."

"Well, as somebody who was a few feet from her when she was still alive I can tell you she was doing her best to remain in this vale of tears."

"What a happy phrase! Vale of tears indeed!"

"You said it." I was disgusted. "Did you tell the police you thought she intended to drown on purpose?"

"Why certainly." Miss Lung was bland. I understood then the promptness of the autopsy. "It was my
duty as a citizen and as a friend of poor Mildred to set
the record straight."

"I hope you're right . . . I mean, in what you did."

"I'm sure I am. Didn't you think that man from the
papers *awfully* distinguished-looking? Not at all my
idea of the usual sort of newspaperman. . . ."

A telephone call from Liz broke short this little chat.
I took it in the hall.

"Peter?"

"That's right. Liz?"

"What on earth is going on over there? Are you all
right?"

"It didn't happen to me."

"Well, you should hear the stories going around. Just
what did happen?"

"One of the guests . . . Mildred Brexton, drowned
this morning."

"Oh, isn't that awful! And on a week end too."

I thought this a strange distinction but let it go. "The
place is a madhouse."

"She's not the painter's wife, is she?"

When I said she was, Liz whistled inelegantly into
the phone, nearly puncturing my eardrum. People like
Brexton are the fragile pillars on which the fashion
world is built.

"That should make quite a splash."

I agreed. "Anyway I'm coming to the dance tonight.
The others are staying in but I'm to be allowed out."

"Oh good! I'll leave an invitation at the front door
for you. Isn't it terribly interesting?"

"You might call it that. See you later."

As I hung up, Mrs. Veering sailed slowly into view,
gliding down the staircase with a priestess-smile on her
lips. She was loaded to the gills.

"Ah, there you are, Peter." For some reason her usually strong voice was pitched very low, gently hushed

as though in a temple. "I understand we've been be-
sieged by members of the press."

"Quite a few. More than you'd expect for a run-of-
the-mill accident."

Mrs. Veering, catching a glimpse of Mary Western
Lung in the drawing room, indicated for me to follow
her out onto the porch where we could be alone with
the twilight. The beach looked lonely and strange in the
light of early evening.

"Do you think I should give an exclusive interview
to Cholly Knickerbocker or one of those people?" She
looked at me questioningly; her face was very flushed
and I wondered if she might not have high blood pres-
sure as well as alcohol in her veins.

"Has he . . . or they asked you for one?"

"No, but I'm sure they will. We've been getting, as
you say, an unusual amount of attention."

"I don't see it'd do any harm. I'd say that Knickerbocker would come under the heading of the right sort
of publicity."

"So should I. My only fear is people will think me
heartless in giving a Labor Day party so close to my
niece's death."

"I wouldn't think so," I said soothingly: I had a
pleasant week or two around Easthampton not to mention a salary to think of. I had no intention of letting
Mrs. Veering give up her party at this stage of the
game. "They'll all understand. Also, they'll be impressed by the publicity."

"Poor Mildred." With that eccentric shift of mood
which I'd noticed earlier, Mrs. Veering had changed
from calm rational matron to Niobe, weeping over her
children, if that's the one who wept over her children.
She stood there beside me, quite erect, the tears stream-
ing down her face. It was unnerving. Then, as suddenly
as it started, her weeping ended and she wiped her
eyes, blew her nose and in her usual voice said, "I
think you're absolutely right. I'll have the invitations
sent out Monday come hell or high water."

Considering the nature of her niece's death, I

thought "high water" inapt but what the hell. "There's one thing I think I should tell you," I said, stopping her as she was about to go into the house.

"Yes?" she paused in the doorway.

"Your friend Miss Lung told the police she thought Mrs. Brexton drowned herself on purpose."

"Oh, no!" Mrs. Veering was shocked into some semblance of normality. "She didn't! She couldn't!"

"She did and she could. I found out when she cornered one of the newsmen a little while ago."

The angry alcoholic flush flickered in her cheeks, mottling them red and white. "How could she?" She stood weakly at the door.

I was soothing: "I don't suppose it'll do much harm. Nobody can prove it one way or the other unless of course there was a last message of some kind."

"But to have people say that ... to say Mildred ... oh, it's going to be awful." And Mrs. Veering, having said that mouthful, made straight for the drawing room and Miss Lung. I went upstairs to change for dinner.

4

I have my best ideas in the bathtub ... at least those that don't come to me unheralded in another part of the bathroom where, enthroned, I am master of the universe.

As I crawled into the old-fashioned bathtub, a big porcelain job resembling an oversize Roman coffin, I thought seriously of what had happened, of the mystery which was beginning to cloud the air.

It's a temptation to say that, even then, I knew the answer to the puzzle but honesty compels me to admit that I was way off in my calculations. Without going into hindsight too much, my impressions were roughly these: Mildred Brexton had had a nervous breakdown for reasons unknown (if any); there was some relationship between Claypoole and her which Brexton knew about and disliked; there were indications that Brexton might have wanted his wife dead; there was definite evidence he had attacked her recently, bruising her neck ... all the relationships of course were a tangle, and no concern of mine. Yet the possibility that Mildred had been murdered was intriguing. I am curious by nature. Also I knew that if anything mysterious *had* happened I would be able to get the beat on every newspaper in New York for the glory of the *N.Y. Globe*, my old paper, and myself. I decided, all things considered, that I should do a bit of investigating. Justice didn't concern me much. But the puzzle, the danger, the excitement of following a killer's trail was all I needed to get involved. Better than big-game hunting, and much more profitable ... if I didn't get killed myself in the process.

I made up my mind to get the story, whatever it was, before the week end was over. I nearly did too.

I dressed and went downstairs.

Our doughty crew was gathered in the drawing room, absorbing gin.

To my surprise Brexton was on hand, looking no different than he had the night before when he made martinis. In fact, he was making them when I joined the party.

Everyone was on his best graveyard behavior. Gloom hovered in the air like a black cloud. I waded through it to the console where Brexton stood alone, the noise of the cocktail shaker in his hands the only sound in the room as the guests studiously avoided each other's gaze.

"What can I do you for?" were, I'm afraid, the first words the bereaved husband said to me when I joined him. For a moment I had a feeling that this was where I came in: his tone was exactly the same as the night before.

"A martini," I said, reliving the earlier time. I half expected to see his wife examining art books on the table opposite but tonight her absence was more noticeable than her presence had been the evening before. He poured me one with a steady hand. "I want to thank you," he said in a low voice, "for handling the press."

"I was glad to."

"I'm afraid I wasn't in any shape to talk to them. Were they pretty bad?"

I wondered what he meant by that, what he wanted to know. I shook my head. "Just routine questions."

"I hope there wasn't any talk of ... of suicide." He looked at me sharply.

"No, it wasn't mentioned. They accepted the fact it was an accident." I paused: then I decided to let him in on Miss Lung's dereliction.

He nodded grimly when I told him what she'd said to the police. "I already know," he said quietly. "They asked me about it and I told them I sincerely doubted Mildred had any intention of killing herself. It's not a very sensible way, is it? Drowning in front of a half-dozen people, several of whom are good swimmers." I was surprised at his coolness. If he was upset by her death, he certainly didn't show it. A little chilled, I joined the others by the fireplace.

Dinner was not gala. Because Brexton was with us we didn't know quite what to talk about. Everybody was thinking about the same thing yet it would've been bad form to talk about Mildred in front of her husband; he of course was the most relaxed of the lot.

It was interesting to note how the different guests reacted to the situation.

Mary Western Lung was deliberately cheery, full of "Book-Chat," discussing at some length a visit she'd once paid Francine Karpin Lock, another noted pen-woman, in the latter's New Orleans' house. "The spirit of graciousness. And her table! Ah, what viands she offers the humblest guest!" This was followed by a close new-critical analysis of her works as compared to those of another great authoress, Taylor Caldwell. I gathered they were neck and neck, artistically speaking, that is.

Mrs. Veering spoke of the Hamptons, of local gossip, of who was leaving her husband for what other man: the sort of thing which, next to children and servant troubles, most occupies the conversation of East-hamptoners.

Fletcher Claypoole said not a word; he was pale and intense and I could see his sister was anxious. She watched him intently all through dinner and though she and I and Brexton carried on a triangular conversation about painting, her attention was uneasily focused on her brother.

Out of deference to the situation, Mrs. Veering decided against bridge though why I'll never know. I should've thought any diversion would have been better than this glum company. I began to study the clock over the mantel. I decided that exactly ten o'clock I'd excuse myself; go upstairs; change, sneak back down and walk the half mile to the Club and Liz and a night of sexual bliss as Marie C. Stopes would say.

My sexual bliss was postponed, however, by the rude arrival of the police.

The butler, quite shaken, ushered a sloppy small man, a detective Greaves, and two plain-clothes men into the drawing room.

Consternation would be a mild word to describe the effect they made.

"Mrs. Veering?" Greaves looked at Miss Lung.

"I am Rose Clayton Veering," said herself, rising shakily from an armchair and crossing the room with marvelous control: I'd counted her drinks that evening: she was not only loaded but primed.

"I'm detective Greaves, ma'am. Bureau of Criminal Investigation."

Miss Lung squeaked disconcertingly; it sounded like a mouse and startled us all. I glanced at Brexton and saw him shut his eyes with resignation.

"Pray, follow me in here, Mr. Graves."

"Greaves." He followed her into the alcove; his two men withdrew to the hall. The guests, myself included, sat in a stunned circle. No one said anything. Claypoole poured himself a drink. Miss Lung looked as though she were strangling. Allie watched her brother

49

as usual and Brexton remained motionless in his chair, his face without expression, his eyes shut.

From the alcove there was a murmur of talk. I could hear Mrs. Veering's voice, indignant and emphatic, while the detective's voice was stern . . . what they said, though, we could not hear. We found out soon enough.

Mrs. Veering, her face flaming with anger, appeared in the door of the alcove accompanied by the policeman who looked a bit sheepish.

"Mr. Graves has something to say to us . . . something so ridiculous that . . ."

"Greaves, ma'am." He interrupted her pleasantly. "Please sit down," he said, indicating a chair. She did as he directed, controlling herself with some effort.

The detective looked at us thoughtfully. He was a sandy-haired little man with red-rimmed eyes and a pale putty face: he looked as though he never slept. But he seemed to have the situation, such as it was, well in hand.

"I hate to come barging in on you like this," he said softly, apologetically. "I've got a list of names and I wish, as I read them off, you'd answer to your name so I'll know which is which." He ran through our names and we answered, Miss Lung startling us again with her shrill mouse-in-terrible-agony squeak.

"Thanks a lot," he said when he'd finished roll call. He was careful not to stare at any one of us too hard or too long. He kept his eyes for the most part on the doorway to the hall.

"Now I won't keep you in the dark any longer. There is a chance that Mrs. Brexton was murdered this morning."

Not a sound greeted this news. We stared back at him, too stunned to comment.

He was disappointed not to have made a different effect. I could see he'd expected some kind of a rise, a significant outburst; instead he got deep silence. This gang was smarter than he'd thought, than I'd thought. I glanced rapidly at the faces but could see nothing more than intense interest in any of them.

When this had been allowed to sink in, he went on softly, "We're not sure of course. It's a queer kind of case. This afternoon an autopsy was performed and it was discovered that the deceased died by drowning; there was no question of a heart attack or of any other physical failure. Her internal organs were sound and undiseased. She was apparently in good physical condition. . . ."

"Then how could she've drowned like that since she was a first-rate swimmer?" Claypoole's voice was tense with strain: it came surprisingly clear across the room.

Greaves looked at him with mild interest. "That's why we're here, Mr. . . . Claypoole. There was apparently *no* reason for her to drown so quickly so near shore with three people attempting rescue. . . ."

"Unless she wanted to," Miss Lung's voice was complacent; she was beginning to recover her usual composure and confidence.

"That is a possibility . . . I *hope* a probability. It is the alternative we'd like to accept. Otherwise, I'm afraid we're stuck with a murder by party or parties unknown."

There it was. Mrs. Veering rallied first. "Mr. Greaves, this is all supposition on your part, and very dangerous too. Regardless of what you might think, there is no evidence that my niece wanted to drown herself nor is there the faintest possibility anybody murdered her. She was in a peculiar mental state as the result of a nervous breakdown. . . . I told you all that a few minutes ago . . . in her condition she was quite apt to lose her head, to drown in that terrible undertow." I was surprised at Mrs. Veering's sharpness. She was completely sobered now and all her usual vagueness and nonsense had been replaced by a steely clarity, and anger.

"An intelligent analysis." Greaves nodded approvingly, as though a favorite pupil had come through. "That was our opinion too when the death was reported this morning. Almost every day there's something like this in these parts, a sudden drowning. Unfortunately

51

the autopsy revealed something odd. It seems that before going in swimming, immediately *after* breakfast, Mrs. Brexton took four sleeping pills . . . or was given four sleeping pills."

This time the silence was complete. No one said anything. Mrs. Veering opened her mouth to speak; then shut it again, like a mackerel on dry land.

"With Mrs. Veering's permission, I'd like to have the house searched for the bottle which contained the pills."

Our hostess nodded, too dazed for words. Greaves poked his head into the hall and said, "O.K., boys." The boys started their search of the house.

"Meanwhile," continued the detective, "I'd appreciate it if everyone remained in this room while I interview you all, individually." He accepted our silence as agreement. To my surprise, he motioned to me. "You'll be first, Mr. Sargeant," he said. I followed him into the alcove. Behind us a sudden buzz of talk, like a hive at swarming time, broke upon the drawing room: indignation, alarm, fear.

He asked me the routine questions and I gave him the routine answers.

Then he got down to the case in hand. At this point, I was still undecided as to what I wanted to do. My mind was working quickly. I've done a few pieces for the *N.Y. Globe* since I left them and I knew that I could get a nice sum for any story I might do on the death of Mildred Brexton; at the same time, there was the problem of Mrs. Veering and my business loyalty to her. This was decidedly the kind of publicity which would be bad for her. I was split down the middle trying to figure what angle to work. While answering his questions, I made an important decision: I decided to say nothing of the quarrel I'd overheard between Brexton and Claypoole. This, I decided, would be my ace-in-the-hole if I should decide to get a beat on the other newspaper people. All in all, I made a mistake.

"Now, Mr. Sargeant, you have, I gather, no real connection with any of these people, is that right?"

I nodded. "Never saw any of them until last night."

"Your impression then should be useful, as an un-prejudiced outsider . . . assuming you're telling us the truth." The detective smiled sadly at me.

"I understand all about perjury," I said stuffily.

"I'm very glad," said the officer of the law gently. "What then was your impression of Mrs. Brexton when you first saw her?"

"A fairly good-looking, disagreeable woman, very edgy."

"Was anything said about her nervous breakdown?"

I nodded. "Yes, it was mentioned, to explain her conduct which was unsocial, to say the least."

"Who mentioned it to you?" He was no clod; I began to have a certain respect for him. I could follow his thought; it made me think along lines that hadn't occurred to me before.

"Mrs. Veering, for one, and Miss Claypoole for another and, I think, Miss Lung said something about it too."

"Before or after the . . . death?"

"Before, I think. I'm not sure. Anyway I did get the impression pretty quick that she was in a bad way mentally and had to be catered to. It all came out in the open the night before she died, when there was some kind of scene between her and her husband." I told him about the screams, about Mrs. Veering's coming to us with soothing words. He took all this down without comment. I couldn't tell whether it was news to him or not. I assumed it was since he hadn't interviewed any of the others yet. I figured I'd better tell him this since he would hear it soon enough from them. I was already beinning to think of him as a competitor. In the past I'd managed, largely by accident, to solve a couple of peculiar crimes. This one looked promising; it was certainly bewildering enough.

"No one actually *saw* Mrs. Brexton screaming?"

"We all heard her. I suppose her husband must've been with her and I think maybe Mrs. Veering was there too, though I don't know. She seemed to be coming from their bedroom, from downstairs, when she told us not to worry."

"I see. Now tell me about this morning."

I told him exactly what had happened: how Brexton got to Mildred first and then nearly drowned himself; how Claypoole pulled her to shore; how I rescued Brexton.

He took all this down without comment. I could see he was wondering the same thing I'd begun to wonder: had Brexton had a chance to pull his wife under just before we got there? I couldn't be absolutely sure because the surf had been in my eyes most of the way out and I hadn't been able to see properly. I doubted it . . . if only because, when I reached them, Brexton was still several feet from his wife who was already half-dead. That Claypoole might have drowned her on the long pull back to shore was an equal possibility but I didn't mention it to Greaves who didn't ask me either. He was only interested in getting the eyewitness part straight.

I asked a question then: "Just what effect would four sleeping pills have . . . four of the kind she took? Are they fatal?"

He looked at me thoughtfully as though wondering whether to bother answering or not. Finally, he said: "They weren't enough to kill her. Make her weak, though, groggy . . . they slowed down the beating of the heart."

"Well, that explains the funny way she swam. I thought the others were just sounding off when they said she was such a fine athlete. She almost fell on her face in her first dive into the surf and her strokes were all off . . . even I could tell that and I'm no coach."

"There's no doubt she died as a result of weakness. She wasn't strong enough to get out of the undertow. The question of course is why, if she'd taken the pills herself, would she've gone in the water instead of to bed where she belonged?"

"To kill herself?" This was the puzzle, I knew.

"A possibility."

"But then somebody might've slipped her those pills, knowing she would probably go swimming."

"Another possibility." Greaves was enigmatic.

"But how could anybody count on that happening? She wasn't feeling well ... maybe she would've just stayed on the shore in the sun. From what I saw of her that would've been *my* guess. I was even surprised, now that I look back, that she went in the ocean at all."

"The person who gave her the pills might have known her better than you. He might've known she would go in the water no matter what her condition." Greaves made notes while he talked.

"And the person who knew her best was, of course, her husband."

Greaves looked at me steadily, "I didn't say that."

"Who else? Even so, if I were Brexton and I wanted to kill my wife, I wouldn't do it like that, with everybody else around."

"Fortunately, you're not Brexton." The coldness in his voice gave me all the clue I needed. The police thought Brexton had killed his wife. I don't know why but even then I didn't think he was responsible. I suppose because my mind dislikes the obvious even though the obvious, as any detective will tell you, nine times out of ten provides the answer.

I threw one last doubt in his path. "Why, if somebody was going to give her the pills, didn't they give her a fatal dose?"

"We must find that out." Greaves was reasonable, polite, bored with me.

Wanting to attract his attention for future need, I said, coolly, "I'll be writing about all this for the *New York Globe*."

This had the effect I intended. He winced visibly. "I thought you were in public relations, Mr. Sargeant."

"I used to be on the *Globe*. In the last few years I've done some features for them. I guess you remember that business a couple of years back when Senator Rhodes was murdered. . . ."

Greaves looked at me with some interest. "You're *that* fellow? I remember the case."

"I was, if I say so myself, of some use to the police."

"That wasn't the way I heard it."

This was irritating. "Well, no matter how you heard it, I intend to do a series on this case for the *Globe,* assuming there really was a murder done, which I doubt."

"Very interesting." Greaves looked at me calmly. At that moment one of the policemen came in and whispered something in his ear. Greaves nodded and the other handed him a handkerchief containing two small cylindrical objects. The policeman withdrew.

"Sleeping pill containers?" I guessed that one right.

He nodded, carefully opening the handkerchief. "As a professional journalist and amateur sleuth, Mr. Sargeant, you should be interested to know that they were found in two places: one bottle in Mrs. Brexton's jewel box; the other in Fletcher Claypoole's bathroom. Both contain the same barbiturate found in Mrs. Brexton's system. Our problem is to determine, if possible, from which bottle the pills she took (or was given) came."

"Just like spin-the-bottle, isn't it?"

"That will be all, Mr. Sargeant."

I had one more shot to fire. I let him have it: "The bruise on Mrs. Brexton's neck was made *before* she went swimming. I noticed it last night at dinner."

"You're very observant, Mr. Sargeant. Thank you."

56

Chapter Three

1

Shortly after one o'clock, I sneaked down the back-stairs of the house, across the deserted kitchen and out the back door. The policeman on guard was faced the other way, sprawled in a wicker armchair at the corner of the house. I ducked down behind the dunes, cursing the clear black night in which the moon rode like a searchlight, casting dense shadows across the dunes, scattering silver light on the cold sea.

I made it to the road, however, without being observed. We'd all been told to remain in the house until further notice and I'd excused myself as soon as possible and gone up to bed, praying the dance wouldn't be over yet.

It wasn't.

Easthampton is a funny place with any number of sets, each mutually exclusive. The center of the village's summer life of course is the group of old-timers who belong to the Ladyrock Yacht Club, a rambling building with a long pier, situated a mile or so north of Mrs. Veering's house, on the road to Ammagansett.

Members of the Club are well-to-do (but not wealthy) socially accepted (but not quite "prominent") of good middle-class American stock (proud of their ancient lineage which goes back usually to some eighteenth-century farmer). Their names are not known to the general public yet they feel that America is a pyramid at the apex of which will be found themselves, a delusion nurtured by the fact that they are not accepted by the rich and the great while they refuse to associate with those poorer than themselves. Their favorite word, however, their highest praise is "nice." You hear that word every few minutes in their company. So-and-so is nice while somebody else isn't. They have divided the world neatly between the nice and the not-nice and they're pretty happy with their side of the border.

Part of being nice means you belong to the club and deplore the presence in the community of such un-nice elements as Jews, artists, fairies and celebrities, four groups which, given half a chance, will, they feel, sweep all that's nice right out to sea. Fortunately the other elements are not conscious of them; otherwise, there could be trouble in this divided village.

As it is, the painters and such like mind their own business in the south end of the town while their nicer neighbors live contentedly together in big houses and small cottages near the Ladyrock; they go to the John Drew Theater in the town; they give parties for one another where at least half the guests get drunk and the other half get offended; they swap wives and husbands while their children coast around at great speed in new cars from Hampton to Hampton wrapping themselves periodically around telephone poles. A typical resort community, and a nice one.

The clubhouse was lighted with Japanese lanterns. A good band was playing. College boys and girls were necking on the dark pier which extended out into the sea. After a fumble with a pile of cards at the door, I was let in to join the nice people who were, all in all, a fairly handsome crew, divided evenly between the well-groomed, well-fed, middle-aged and the golden

young on their summer vacation. The middle generation, mine, were all off working to make enough
money to get a summer place out here and, at forty, to
join the Ladyrock Yacht Club.

Liz found me at the bar where I was ordering a
Manhattan and hoping she'd come along to sign for it.

She was beautiful, in black and white with something
or other shining in her hair: her eyes glittered and she
was pleasantly high.

"Oh, it's wonderful you got away! I was afraid you
wouldn't be able to." She signed for my drink like a
good girl. "Come on, let's dance."

"Not until I've had this."

"Well, come on out on the pier then. I want to talk
to you." We made our way slowly across the dance
floor. Young and old bucks pawed Liz who apparently
was the belle of this ball. Several old school friends of
mine, bald and plump (guests like myself; not yet
members) greeted me and I knew at least a dozen of
the girls, which Liz didn't like.

"You're such a flirt," she said, once we were on the
pier. The moon shone white upon our heads. The
young lovers were farther out the pier. A number of alcoholics reeled cheerfully along the boardwalk which
separated the pier from the club itself.

"I've just been around a long time."

But she was more interested in the murder. And she
knew it was murder. "It's all over town!" she said ex-
citedly. "Everybody says Brexton drowned her."

"I wonder how that rumor started?" I hedged.

"Oh, *you* know and you won't tell me." She looked
at me accusingly. "I promise I won't breathe a word to
anybody."

"On your honor as a Girl Guide?"

"Oh, Peter, tell me! You were there. You saw it happen, didn't you?"

"I saw it happen all right." I put my empty glass
down on the railing and put one arm around her; she
shook away.

"You *have* to tell," she said.

59

"Don't I appeal to you?"

"Men don't appeal to women, as you well know," she said loftily. "We are only interested in homemaking and, on top of that, our sexual instinct does not fully develop until the late twenties. I'm too young to have any responses."

"But I'm too old. The male, as we all know, reaches his sexual peak at sixteen after which he declines steadily into a messy old age. I am long past my prime ... an erotic shell capable of only a minor. . . ."

"Oh, Peter, tell me or I'll scream!" Her curiosity brought an end to our Kinseyan dialogue. It has recently become the aim of our set to act entirely in accordance with the master's findings and what the majority do and feel we do and feel, more or less. I was all ready to launch into the chapter on premarital petting which leads to climax but not penetration; unfortunately my companion, deeply interested in murder like any healthy girl, had begun to scream.

"For God's sake, shut up!" I said nervously. Luckily only alcoholics were on the terrace ... a trio of minor executives in minor banks applauded softly her first scream; the couples on the pier were all engaged in premarital petting (college-type) and chose not to hear her.

"You'll tell me?" she took a deep breath, ready for a loud scream.

"There's nothing to tell. Mrs. Brexton took four sleeping pills, went in swimming and drowned before we could get to her."

"*Why* did she take four sleeping pills?"

"That is the question which hovers over all our heads like the sword of Themistocles."

"Damocles," said that classic scholar. "Somebody give her the pills?"

"Who knows."

"She took them herself?"

"So I think, but the police have other ideas."

"Like Paul Brexton giving them to her secretly?"

"Or someone else ... though why the nonfatal four, I'll never know. If he really wanted to do her in, I

should think the usual dozen would have been in order."

"It's all a *devious* plot, Peter. Any fool can see it.
She was going in swimming: what could be smarter
than giving her something to make her groggy just as
she got out in that awful undertow?"

"I can think of a lot of things which'd be smarter.
Among them. . . ." I slipped my arm around her again
but she was extremely unresponsive.

"On the other hand, I don't suppose there was any
way of knowing for sure she *would* go in the water. Oh,
isn't it terribly exciting? And happening to Brexton too,
of all people."

"It will cause unpleasant talk," I said, drawing her
even closer to me: I smelled lilacs and the fresh warm
odor of Liz.

"What on earth do you have in mind Peter?"

"It's not in my mind. . . ."

"Filthy, brutish creatures . . . all men are the same."

"If you'd rather I'll get you a sixteen-year-old boy."

"And what on earth would I do with one of those?"

"Modesty impels me to draw a veil over. . . ."

"It'll be in all the papers, won't it?"

"What? The sixteen-year. . . ."

"No, you idiot, Mrs. Brexton's death."

"Well, of course. . . ."

"Isn't that just wonderful for you? That's your job,
isn't it?"

"I wasn't hired to handle Mrs. Brexton's murder."
As I said this, I was suddenly startled by the implications. It was too wild . . . and yet mightn't Mrs. Veering have suspected there'd be trouble and hired me in
advance, just in case? She was the kind to look ahead:
a combination Hetty Green and lush. The possibility
that *she* might have been the one to ease her niece into
a more beautiful world occurred to me then. Motive
was obscure but then I didn't know anybody's motive
. . . they were all strangers to me. Even so it was the
kind of thing Mrs. Veering *might* do . . . she was both

61

mad and methodical, an unusual combination. The thought was sobering.

Liz noticed my sudden thoughtfulness. "What're you thinking about?" she asked. "Are you considering ways of seducing me?"

I snorted. "What is more ignoble than a woman? You have not the slightest sensual interest in the male, even in such a perfect specimen as myself, yet at all hours of the day and night you think about seduction. . . ."

"And homemaking. A little two-room apartment in Peter Cooper Village. Birdseye products in the frigidaire . . . Clapp's strained baby food on the shelf and a darling fat baby wetting itself periodically in a special fourteen ninety-five Baby-Leroy crib from Macy's."

"My God, you *are* prepared for marriage!"

Liz smiled enigmatically. "We all are. Actually, I'm doing a piece on the young married couple in New York City for one of the magazines, not *Harper's Bazaar*. Something more middle-class. They want me to describe bliss on thirty-five dollars a week. You don't know what a good wife I'll make!"

"There's more to marriage than that."

"Than thirty-five dollars? I suppose there is. I think I'd like someone very rich. But seriously, Peter, you don't really believe Brexton killed his wife, do you? I mean it just isn't the kind of thing that happens."

"I don't know what to think." This was my clearest statement so far, and the most accurate. I then swore her to secrecy and we went back inside.

Everyone was fairly tight. The very nicest people had gone home. Only one stag had been knocked down in the john (you may recall what happened to the late Huey Long in a Long Island men's room some years ago); a husband and wife (another woman's husband, another man's wife) were locked tight together in a dim corner of the room. The college set, a particularly beautiful gang of sunburned animals, were singing songs and feeling each other happily while plotting their next move which, from what I overheard, was an all-out attack on Southampton. Already I could hear the crash of cars into solid objects, the tinkling of broken glass: youth!

And youth, in the congenial form of Liz Bessemer, was all mine that night. Her uncle and aunt had gone home. The various bucks who had been competing for her favors had either gone off with whatever available girls were on hand or had quietly passed out among the parked convertibles.

"Let's go to Montauk!" This brilliant idea came to Liz as we moved slowly around the dance floor, waltzing to a fox trot ... I have no sense of beat and, besides, only know how to waltz which I do fairly well to any music.

"Walking?"

"I'll drive. I've got the car ... at least I think I have. Aunt went home in our house guest's car ... I hope."

Aunt had indeed gone home in the house guest's car, leaving us a fine Buick with its top down.

She leaped into the driver's seat and I relaxed beside her as we drove swiftly down the center of the long straight road which runs parallel to the dunes all the way to Montauk, Long Island's sandy terminus.

The moon almost blinded us; it shone directly in our eyes. We stopped a long way before Montauk. At my direction, we turned off the road and drove down a sandy trail which ended in the Atlantic Ocean. Between two dunes, a mile from the nearest darkened house, we made love.

I've never seen such a night as that one. The sky was filled with all the stars available in that happy latitude while everywhere, in every part of the sky, meteors were falling.

When it was over, we lay side by side on the sand which was still faintly warm from the sun and we looked at the stars, the meteors and the moon. A salt breeze dried our naked bodies. She shivered and I put my arm under her and pulled her close ... she was light in my arms.

"I ought to get back," she said, her voice small, no longer teasing.

"Almost day." We thought about that for a while. She pulled herself up on her elbow and looked at me curiously in the moonlight. "What are you thinking about?" she asked.

"Nothing."

"Tell me."

"Nothing . . . except maybe how pleasant it is on the beach like this and how much I'll hate having to get dressed again and go back to that house."

She sighed and stretched. "It *was* nice, wasn't it?"

I pulled her down on my chest and kissed her for answer; her small breasts tickled my skin. I was ready again even though at my age I'm officially past the peak but she sensed this and, instead, got to her feet and ran down to the water and dove in.

Remembering what had happened less than twenty-four hours before, I was scared to death. I leaped into the cold black water after her. Fortunately, she was a good swimmer and we kept well within the surf line. It was strange, swimming in that black ocean under a black sky . . . the moon and the beach white, and the tops of the waves, bright with phosphorus.

Then, shivering and laughing, we ran back to the car and dried ourselves with her aunt's lap rug.

We both agreed that the other looked just fine with no clothes on and Liz admitted shyly to me that she got a minor thrill out of observing the male body in a state of nature if she liked the person who owned the body. I told her she was unnatural and might end up as a footnote in a textbook.

In a happy mood, we drove south and she let me off a few yards from the North Dunes just as daylight, gray and pink, smudged the east.

"Tomorrow?"

She nodded. "If I can manage it. I don't know what's on."

"I don't either but I can sneak off."

"I can too. I'll call you when I know." We kissed long

and blissfully; then she was gone in a screech of gears. She was one of the worst drivers I've ever known, but she was also a wonderful girl. I experienced an emotion which was something more than my usual athleticism; then I quickly put all romantic thoughts out of my head. She was a lovely girl; the night had been perfect; the moon bright; what should've happened did happen and that was that. I am not the serious kind in these matters, I said to myself sternly as I opened the back door quietly and stepped into the kitchen.

2

I came to in bed.

My head felt as if someone had whetted an axe on it and at first I suffered from double vision. Everything was blurred. Then, with an effort, I brought Mrs. Veering into focus.

She was standing over me, an anxious look on her face. Light streamed in the window.

"What time is it?" I asked.

"Ten o'clock. You certainly had us scared out of our wits! What on earth happened to you?"

I put my hand to my head where an enormous lump had formed. No skin had been broken and there was no bandage, only an aching head. "I haven't any idea. I got home about dawn and. . . ."

Greaves appeared in the doorway. "Has he been conscious long, Mrs. Veering?"

"Just this minute. If you. . . ."

"Could you leave us alone, please: I'd like to ask Mr. Sargeant a few questions."

"Certainly." With a reassuring pat, Mrs. Veering trotted off, shutting the door behind her.

"Well?" the policeman looked at me, half smiling.

"Well what?" I felt awful. I noticed I was wearing only a shirt and shorts. I was suddenly very hot under the blanket. I threw it off and sat up dizzily, swinging my legs over the side of the bed.

"Were you trying to do our job for us, Mr. Sargeant?"

"Go away."

"I'm afraid you must answer my questions. You received a severe blow but according to the doctor there was no concussion and you'll be able to get up whenever you like."

"Would you do me the courtesy of going away and coming back when I feel better?" My head was pounding with pain as I moved shakily toward the bathroom. "I'm about to perform a natural function," I said sharply.

"I can wait."

I groaned and went into the bathroom where I put my head under the cold water tap; then I took two Empirin tablets, figuring if I wasn't supposed to take any I'd have been warned. I was being treated too damn casually, I thought.

When I returned, Greaves was seated in the armchair by my bed, making marks in a small notebook.

"You still here?"

"What happened?" He looked at me expectantly.

"A woman dressed all in black and carrying what seemed to be calla lilies was crossing the kitchen when I entered. When I asked her if I might be of assistance, she brought the lilies down on my head, shrieking 'Thus to all members of the MacTavish Clan!' "

Greaves looked faintly alarmed, as though not sure how serious the blow might have been. "Calla lilies?" he asked.

"Or something." I took my clothes off, hoping that would get rid of him, but he still regarded me with the same abstracted air while I got into a bathing suit.

"You didn't see her face?"

"I am making fun of you," I said, feeling light in the head, as though I'd drunk too much too fast. I sat down weakly on the edge of the bed. "Didn't see anybody. Walked in the kitchen door and bang! That was the end until I just now opened my eyes."

"You were struck from the right side by a metal object held by a person as tall or a little taller than yourself. . . ."

"Or standing on a chair. . . ."

"Or standing on something, yes. You were discovered at seven-thirty by the cook who screamed for four minutes. One of my men brought you up here and a doctor was called."

"No clues?"

"We call them leads, Mr. Sargeant. The police department is not. . . ."

"Then were there any leads? Like a strand of blond hair soaked in blood or maybe the old dandruff of a middle-aged murderer scattered beside my still form?"

"Nothing but your still form was found." He paused, indicating that for his money it wasn't still enough.

"Well, there's nothing more I can say."

"You were out. You left the house after I expressly asked everyone to stay in. You were dressed in a. . . ."

"Tuxedo with a loose inner button. I went to the Ladyrock Yacht Club. . . ."

"After which you and a Miss Liz Bessemer drove north to Amagansett."

This stopped me. "What happened then, in Amagansett?"

"I don't know and I don't care. Miss Bessemer dropped you off here at five-twenty or thereabouts."

"I suppose your man saw all this? The one who was sound asleep when I came home."

"He *was* sound asleep and he's been replaced." Greaves was calm, implacable. "Sargeant, what do you know?"

He whipped this last out like a spray of cold water in my face. He was leaning forward now, intense, grimly serious.

"About what?" The Empirin hadn't begun to work yet and my head ached fiercely.

"You know something you haven't told us, some-

67

thing important . . . you know enough for the murderer to want to kill you."

This had occurred to me some minutes before when I came to, aware I'd been clubbed. I was in the dark, though. I was fairly certain neither Brexton nor Claypoole knew I'd overheard their conversation. They were the likeliest pair.

Greaves was on a different tack, however. I found out soon enough what was on his mind. "What did you see out there in the water, when Mrs. Brexton was drowning? What did Brexton do exactly? What did Claypoole do? And the woman, did she speak? Did she call for help?"

"You think I saw something out there that somebody . . . the murderer, didn't want me to, is that it?"

"That's it."

I shook my head which was beginning, slowly, to clear. "I've gone over the whole thing a dozen times in my mind since it happened, but I can't find anything unusual . . . anything you don't already know."

"How close was Brexton to his wife when you got to him?"

"About five feet, I'd say . . . not very close. He was gagging and getting blue in the face. I grabbed him while. . . ."

"Claypoole grabbed Mrs. Brexton."

"Yes. Then we came into shore."

"Brexton never touched his wife, did he?"

I shook my head. "I don't think so. The spray was in my eyes. I was bucking surf all the way. When I got there, she was sinking, going down again and again, hardly struggling enough to get herself back up. She didn't make a sound."

"And Claypoole?"

"He was behind me all the way until we finally got out to them: then he spurted on ahead and grabbed Mrs. Brexton. I had my hands full with her husband."

"How did Claypoole handle her on the way in?"

"I wasn't watching. About the same way I managed Brexton . . . standard Junior Life Saver stuff."

Greaves lit a pipe thoughtfully. "He'll try it again."

"Who will try what?"

"The murderer will take another crack at you."

I chuckled, though I didn't feel any too merry. "I don't think that's why I was cracked over the head. After all, if somebody was interested in killing me, he wouldn't rely on one blow to do it. On top of that how'd he know I was going to come creeping into the kitchen at five A.M.? And what was *he* doing there?"

"These are all questions we mean to consider," said Greaves with the slow ponderousness of a public servant out of his depth.

"Well, while you're considering them I'm going to get something to eat, and some sun. I ache all over."

"I'd be very careful if I were you, Mr. Sargeant."

"I'll do my best. You might keep your boys on the alert, too."

"I intend to. There's a murderer in this house, Mr. Sargeant, and it's my opinion he's after you."

"You make me feel like a clay pigeon."

"I think bait is a better word, don't you?" He was a cold bastard.

3

I got some breakfast on the porch where I held court, surrounded by the ladies of the party to whom I was something of a hero. Claypoole it seemed was in Easthampton and Brexton was in his room painting . . . though where he'd get enough light I didn't know, glancing at the window near the chair where I sat with the ladies, aware that everything we said could be heard by anyone in that room.

It was Mary Western Lung who most appreciated my situation. She was in her yellow slacks; her harlequin glasses, adorned with rhinestones, glittered in the sun which streamed across the porch. "We all came running when the cook started carrying on. You never *saw* such a commotion ... you looked so dead, there on the floor. *I* called for a doctor," she added, to show that hers was the clearest head.

"Did you get a glimpse of who did it?" Allie Claypoole was gratifyingly tense.

"No, nothing at all. When I opened the door to the kitchen somebody slugged me."

Mrs. Veering stirred her orange juice with her forefinger: I wondered what pale firewater it contained, probably gin, the breakfast drink. "The police requested us all to keep quiet about this," she said. "I can't think why. My theory is that we had a prowler ... there's one loose in Southampton, you know. I think he stumbled in here; when he heard you he was frightened and. . . ."

"And tiptoed quietly home, past a sleeping policeman on the front porch?" I shook my head. "I don't think a run-of-the-mill burglar would go anywhere near a house with a policeman standing guard, even a sleeping one."

The others agreed. Mrs. Veering preferred her theory, though. The alternative made everybody nervous.

It was Miss Lung who said what we were thinking: "Somebody in this house wanted to ... rub out Mr. Sargeant." She paused, eyes wide, obviously pleased with "rub out."

"The murderer," I said agreeably, "obviously thinks I know something." As I talked I was aware of that open window two yards away, of Brexton listening. "I don't of course. The whole thing's . . ."

"A nightmare!" Allie was suddenly vehement. "It *couldn't* be more awful, more pointless!"

"I think," said Mrs. Veering sternly, "that everybody tends to jump to conclusions. There's no proof Mildred was murdered. *I* decline to think she was. Certainly no one here would do such a thing and as for Mr. Sargeant . . . well, there *are* other explanations." What they were though she didn't see fit to tell us. She turned accusingly to Mary Western Lung: "And I thought you

70

particularly agreed with me that murder was out of the question."

Miss Lung gestured vaguely with her pincushion of a hand. "What happened to Mr. Sargeant changed my mind. As you know, I felt all along that poor Mildred had every intention of meeting her Maker when she stepped into that water yesterday. But now I'm not so sure."

They argued for some time about what had happened. There were no facts to go on other than my unexpected conjunction with a bit of metal. None of them had, until then, wanted to face the fact that Mildred was murdered. Their reasons were unknown to me ... and their reasons, if ever I could understand them, would provide a key to the tangle. It was precisely at that moment, while drinking coffee and listening to the chatter of three women, that I made up my mind to go after the killer. The fact that he, or she, had gone after me first of course had something to do with my decision: I had no intention of dying in Easthampton that summer.

Mrs. Veering wanted to see me privately after breakfast but I excused myself first to make some telephone calls. I cornered several newspapers and took them up to my room which was now empty. I'm ashamed to confess I looked under the bed and in the closet before locking the door.

Then I read the papers quickly. No mention of murder yet. But the stories hinted at mysteries. *The Daily News* announced that the deceased had had a nervous breakdown and indicated tactfully that suicide was a possibility. That seemed to be the general line in the press. There were some old pictures of Brexton about the time of their marriage, looking very Newport and not very Bohemian. Mrs. Veering was good for a picture in the *Journal* and the *Globe*. This was fine: she was still my client.

I telephoned Miss Flynn, wondering if anybody else was listening on the wire. House-party telephones are notorious: I suspect a great many divorces have occurred as a result of week ends at big houses with a lot of phones, all tuned in on each other.

Miss Flynn was cold. "I assume the late socialite wife of the well-known Modern Painter died a Natural Death?" The skepticism in her voice was heavy enough to cauterize the receiver.

"As far as we know," I said glibly. "Now I may have to stay out here for a week. The police have asked . . ."

"I understand." She was a rock. She cut short any further explanations. "I will carry on at the office as best I can," she said. "I assume you will be in touch with the *Globe*."

"Well, come to think of it, I might give them a ring to find out if they'd like me to do. . . ."

"The Human Interest Angle, I know. I trust you will be cautious in your investigations."

I assured her that I would be. I told her then what I wanted done for our various clients during my absence.

Then I got the managing editor of the *New York Globe* at his home in Westport.

"Good to hear from you, boy. Not mixed up in another murder, are you?"

"Matter of fact I am."

I could hear a quick intake of breath on the other end of the wires: the managing editor was rapidly figuring how cheaply he could buy me. We had done business before. "What's the deal?" he asked, his voice carefully bored.

"Mildred Brexton."

"Easthampton? Are you out there now?"

"In Mrs. Veering's house. I suppose you've been following. . . ."

"Thought it was an accident."

"Police think not. Now. . . ." We haggled like gentlemen and I got my price. I also asked him to get me all the material he could on Mrs. Veering, the Claypooles, the Brextons and Mary Western Lung . . . they were all more or less public figures, either professionally or socially. He said he would and I told him I'd have a story for him in a couple of days, long before the other services had even got an interview out of the principals. I hung up ... a second later I lifted the receiver and heard a click on the wire. Somebody had been listening.

The back of my head was beginning to feel more human though it was still oddly shaped. I went back downstairs. On my way through the hall, Mrs. Veering beckoned to me from the door to the sunroom. I joined her in there. We were alone; the others were out on the beach. The police were nowhere in sight.

"Where's Greaves?" I asked.

"Gone ... for the time being. We have a twenty-four-hour guard, though," she added dramatically. For once the inevitable tumbler of the waters of Lethe was not at hand. I wondered if she was sober; I wondered if there was any way of telling.

"I suppose he's investigating."

"Mr. Sargeant ... Peter, I believe we are all in terrible danger."

I took this calmly enough ... I could even go along with it. "Doesn't seem to be anything we can do about it," I said noncommittally.

"There must be!" She clasped and unclasped her hands nervously.

"I thought you felt it was all an accident, that I was slugged by a prowler and. ..."

"I didn't want to upset the others. I didn't want them to know that I *knew*." She looked at me darkly.

"Knew what?"

"That there is danger."

I decided she was off her rocker, or else *did* know something the rest of us didn't. "Have you told the police?"

"I can't tell them anything. It's only a ... presentiment."

"Do you or don't you think Mrs. Brexton was murdered?"

She would not answer; instead she just sighed and looked out the window at the velvety green golf course,

73

brilliant as a pool table in the light of noon. She changed the subject with that rapidity which I was finally getting used to; alcoholics find any train of thought too long sustained tiring: "I want you to mention my Labor Day party in your first dispatch to the *Globe*." She smiled at me.

"You were listening on the phone?"

"Say that a little bird told me." She was coy.

"You don't mind my writing about the murder?"

"Of course I mind but since everyone else will be writing about it in those *awful* tabloids it'll be to my advantage to have you here in the house, a gentleman." Her realism always surprised me.

"I was afraid you might be upset."

"Not at all, but I'd like to see what you write from time to time. I may be able to help you."

"That'd be awfully nice of you."

"Not at all."

"*Was* your niece murdered?" I asked suddenly, trying to catch her off guard.

"You'll get no help from me there." And that was the end of that interview: I left her for the beach and the sun.

I found only Allie Claypoole on the beach.

She was lying on her back in a two-piece red bathing suit which was exciting to contemplate: I found her most attractive and if it hadn't been for my fling with Liz the night before and the peculiar discovery that, despite a lifetime devoted to philandering, I was unexpectedly held to the idea of Liz, and didn't want anybody else, not even the slender Allie who looked up at me with a smile and said, "Recovered?"

I sat down beside her on the sand. The sun was soothing. The sea sparkled. Just twenty-four hours ago it had happened. "I feel much better. Where's everybody?"

"Miss Lung has gone inside to write this week's 'Book-Chat' while my brother's in town. Brexton's in his room still. What on earth is going on?"

I gestured helplessly. "I haven't any idea. I never

74

saw any of these people before Friday. *You* ought to know."

"I can't make any sense out of it." She rubbed oil on her brown arms.

"Mrs. Veering feels we are all in terrible danger."

Allie smiled wanly. "I'm afraid Rose always feels she's in great danger, especially when she's been drinking."

"She seemed quite sober this morning."

"You never can tell. I wouldn't take anything she says too seriously. It's all part of her own private madness."

"On the other hand that knock on the head I got this morning was not just one of her hallucinations."

"No, that's more serious. Even so I can't really believe anybody killed Mildred . . . not one of us, that is. This is the sort of thing which is supposed to happen to other people."

"What do *you* think happened?" I looked at her innocently: I had to pump these people, one by one. The best approach was bewildered stupidity.

"I believe what Paul says."

This was news; I hadn't known that Brexton had expressed himself yet on the murder, except perhaps to the police. "What does he say?"

"That Mildred was in the habit of taking sleeping pills at all hours of the day, to calm her nerves. That the ones she took the morning she died were a standard dose for her and that she went in swimming not realizing how tough the undertow was."

"Well, it sounds sensible."

"Except that my brother had a bottle of the same type pills. . . ."

"You don't mean they suspect him?"

She shook her head, her face grim. "No, I don't think they do. He had no motive and even if he did there's no proof the pills came from him. Their idea seems to be that somebody might have had access to his bathroom who didn't have access to Mildred's pills which were kept locked in her jewel box: she was the only one who knew the combination. Brexton swears *he* never knew it and couldn't have got the thing open if he wanted to."

"So either she got the pills herself or somebody went into your brother's bathroom and got some to put in her coffee or whatever it was she took them in?"

"That's the general line. If you hadn't been attacked last night, I'd have thought Mildred took the pills herself. Now I'm not sure."

"It looks like my adventure may have started the whole thing rolling."

She nodded. "I thought that awful little man Graves, or whatever his name is, was just trying to scare us, to get himself attention. I still don't think he has the vaguest idea whether or not a murder was committed."

"He's fairly sure now. Are you?"

"I don't know what to think."

"What was between your brother and Mildred?" I asked this all in one breath to take her by surprise; it did.

Her eyelids fluttered with alarm; she frowned, taken aback. "What ... what makes you think anything. ..."

"Mrs. Veering," I lied. "She told me that, years ago. ..."

"That bloody fool!" She literally snarled; but then she was in control again. She even managed to laugh convincingly to cover up her sudden lapse. "I'm sorry," she said quickly. "It just seems so unnecessary, raking up family skeletons. The facts are simple enough: Mildred was engaged to marry my brother. Then she met Brexton and married him instead. That's all. My brother was devoted to her and not too friendly with Brexton, though they got on ... that's all there is to it."

"Why didn't she marry your brother?"

She was evasive. "I suppose Brexton was more glamorous to her. ..."

"Did *you* like the idea of his marrying her?"

"I can't think that that has anything to do with it, Mr. Sargeant." She looked at me coldly.

"I suppose it doesn't. I'm sorry. It's just that if I'm

to be used as a punching bag by a murderer, I'd like to know a little something about what's going on."

"I'm sorry." She was quick to respond. "I didn't mean to be unpleasant. It's just that it's a sore subject with all of us. In fact, I didn't even want to come down here for the week end but Fletcher insisted. He was very fond of Mildred, always."

I was slowly getting an idea of the relationships involved, as much from what she didn't say as what she did.

The butler called me from the terrace. Liz was on the telephone. I answered it in the hall.

"Darling, are you all right?" Her voice was anxious.

"Don't tell me you heard. . . ."

"Everything! My aunt told me this morning how, when you came home last night, you were *stabbed*. I've been trying to get you for two hours but the line's been busy. Are you all right? Where. . . ."

I told her what had happened, marveling at the speed with which news spread in that community. I supposed the servants had passed it on since I knew no one in the house, none of the guests, would have breathed a word of it.

She was relieved that I hadn't been stabbed. She was also alarmed. "I don't think you should stay another night in that awful place, Peter. No, I mean it, really. It's perfectly apparent that a criminal maniac is on the loose and. . . ."

"And when do I see you?"

"Oh. Well, what about late tonight? Around midnight. I'm tied up with the family till then but afterward I'm invited to Evan Evans' house . . . the abstract sculptor. I could meet you there. It's open house." I took down the address and then, after promising her I wouldn't get in the way of any more metal objects, she rang off.

I wandered back to the beach. From upstairs I could hear the clatter of Mary Western Lung's feverish typewriter. The door to Brexton's room was shut. Mrs. Veering was writing letters in the sunroom.

Everything was peaceful. Allie Claypoole was talking to a stranger when I rejoined her on the beach. "Oh, Mr. Sargeant, I want you to meet Dick Randan ... he's my nephew."

The nephew was a tall gangling youth of twenty odd summers: he wore heavy spectacles and a seersucker suit which looked strangely out of place on that glaring beach. I made the expected comment about what a young aunt Allie was, and she agreed.

"Dick just drove down from Cambridge today. . . ."

"Heard what had happened and came down to make sure everything was all right." His voice was as unprepossessing as the rest of him. He sat like a solemn owl on the sand, his arms clasping bony knees. "Just now got here ... quite a row," he shook his head gloomily. "Bad form, this," he added with considerable understatement.

"Dick's taking his Master's degree in history," said Allie as though that explained everything. "You better run in the house, dear, and tell Rose you're here."

"Oh, I'll stay in the village," said the young historian.

"Well, go in and say hello anyway. I'm sure she'll ask you to dinner."

Wiping sand off his trousers, the nephew disappeared into the house. Allie sighed, "I should've known Dick would show up. He loves disaster. I suppose it's why he majored in history ... all those awful wars and things."

"Maybe he'll cheer us up."

"It'll take more than Dick I'm afraid."

"You're not much older than he, are you?"

She smiled. "Now that's what I call a nice thing to hear. Yes, I'm a good ten years older." Which made her thirty one or two, I figured with one of those rapid mental computations which earned me the reputation of a mathematical failure in school.

Then we went in swimming, keeping close to shore.

4

Miss Lung and I were the first to arrive for cocktails. Her dress made her look even more repellent than usual. She thought she was cute as a button though.

"Well, looks like we're the first down. The vanguard." I gave her a drink and agreed. I sat down opposite her though she'd done everything but pull me down beside her on the couch. I realize that, contrary to popular legend, old maids' traditional lechery is largely an invention of the male but I can safely say that, in Miss Lung's case, masculine irreverence was justified.

She sipped her martini; then, after spilling half of it on the rug, put it down and said, "I hope you're recovered from your encounter with that unknown party."

I said I was.

"I could hardly keep my mind on 'Book-Chat.' I was doing a piece on how strange it is that all the best pen-women with the possible exception of Taylor Caldwell possess three names."

I let the novelty of this pass. I was saved from any further observations by the appearance of Claypoole. He was pale and preoccupied. He looked as though he hadn't slept in a week.

He made conversation mechanically. "The whole town's buzzin'," he said. "I was down at the theater seeing the pictures there ... some good things, too, by the way, though of course Paul would say they're trash."

"What's trash? What would I call trash?" Brexton appeared in the doorway; he was even smiling, some of his old geniality returning. I wondered why. At the moment his neck was half inside a noose.

Claypoole looked at him bleakly. "I was talking about the pictures down at the John Drew Theater."

"On, they're trash all right," said Brexton cheerfully, mixing himself a drink. "You're absolutely right, Fletcher."

"I liked them. I said you'd say they were. . . ."

"What they are. Well, here's to art!"

"Art? I love it!" Mrs. Veering and Dick Randan came in together; the former was her usual cheery self, high as a kite. She introduced the Claypoole connection to Miss Lung and Brexton neither of whom knew him. The penwoman shifted her affections abruptly from me to the young historian. "So you're at Harvard?" she began to purr and the youth was placed beside her on the couch. That was the end of him for that evening.

Allie was the last to join us. She sat by me. "Well, here we all are," she said irrelevantly.

The company was hectically gay that night. We were all infected by this general mood. Everyone drank too much. I was careful, though, to watch and listen, to observe. I knew that someone in that room had clubbed me with possible intent to kill. But who? And why?

I watched their faces. Brexton was unexpectedly cheerful. I wondered if he'd arranged himself an alibi that afternoon while locked in his room. On the other hand, Claypoole seemed to be suffering. He had taken the death of Mildred harder than anyone. Something about him bothered me. I didn't like him but I didn't know why. Perhaps it was the strange relationship with his sister . . . but that was no business of mine.

Miss Lung responded to whatever was the mood of any group. Her giggles now rose like pale echoes of Valkyrie shrieks over the dinner table while Mrs. Veering, in a mellow state, nodded drunkenly from time to time. Randan stared about him with wide eyes, obviously trying to spot the murderer, uninfected by the manic mood.

It was like the last night of the world.

Even I got a little drunk finally although I'd intended to keep a clear head, to study everyone. Unfortunately, I didn't know what to study.

We had coffee in the drawing room. While I was sitting there, talking absently to the nephew about Harvard, I saw Greaves tiptoe quietly across the hall. I wondered what he was up to.

"Did the murderer really slug you?" asked Randan suddenly, interrupting me in the middle of a tearful story about the old days when Theodore Spencer was alive and Delmore Schwartz and other giants brooded over the university.

"Yes." I was short with him; I was getting tired of describing what had happened to me.

"Then you must possess some sort of information which he wishes to destroy."

"Me? Or the information?" Randan had expressed himself as most history majors do.

"Both, presumably."

"Who knows?" I said. "Anyway he's wasting his time because I don't know a thing."

"It's really quite exciting." His eyes glittered black behind the heavy spectacles. "It presents a psychological problem too. The relationships involved are. . . ." I got away as soon as was decently possible.

I told Mrs. Veering that I was tired and wanted to go to bed early; she agreed, adding it was a wonder I didn't feel worse, considering the blow I'd received.

In the hall I found Greaves. He was sitting in a small upright chair beside the telephone table, a piece of paper in one hand and a thoughtful expression on his face.

"Ready to make an arrest?" I asked cheerfully.

"What? Oh . . . you plan to go out tonight again?"

"Yes, I was going to ask you if it was all right."

"I can't stop you," said Greaves sadly. "Do us a favor, though, and don't mention anything about what's been happening here."

"I can't see that it makes much difference. Papers are full of it."

"They're also full of something else. We have two men on duty tonight," he added.

"I hope that'll be enough."

"If you remember to lock your door."

81

"The murderer might have a key."

"One of the men will be on the landing. His job is to watch your room."

I chuckled. "You don't really think anything will happen with two policemen in the house, do you?"

"Never can tell."

"You don't have any evidence, do you?"

"Not really." The answer was surprisingly frank. "But we know what we're doing."

"As a bit of live bait and a correspondent for the *Globe, what* are you doing?"

"Wouldn't tell you for the world, Mr. Sargeant."

"When do you think you'll make your arrest? There'll be a grand jury soon won't there?"

"Friday, yes. We hope to be ready . . . we call it Special Court, by the way."

"Already drawn up your indictment?"

"Could be. Tell me, Mr. Sargeant, you don't play with paper dolls, do you?"

This set me back on my heels. "Dolls?" I looked at him, at sea.

"Or keep a scrapbook?"

"My secretary keeps a scrapbook, a professional one . . . what're you talking about?"

"Then this should amuse you, in the light of our earlier discussions." He pushed the pieces of paper at me.

It was an ordinary piece of typewriter paper on which had been glued a number of letters taken from headlines: they were all different sizes; they spelled out "Brescton is Ciller."

"When did you get this?"

"I found it right here, this morning." Greaves indicated the telephone table. "It was under the book, turned face down. I don't know how I happened to turn it over . . . looked like scratch paper."

"Then it wasn't sent to you?"

"Nor to anybody. Just put on the table where anyone might find it. Very strange."

"Fingerprints?"

He looked at me pityingly. "Nobody's left a set of

fingerprints since Dillinger. Too many movies. Everybody wears gloves now."

"I wonder why the words are misspelled?"

"No 'X' and not many 'K's' in headlines ... these were all taken from headlines apparently. Haven't figured out which paper yet."

"Who do you think left it there?"

"You." He looked at me calmly.

I burst out laughing. "If I thought Brexton was the murderer I'd tell you so."

Greaves shrugged. *"Don't* tell me. It's your neck, Mr. Sargeant."

"Just why would I want to keep anything like that a secret?"

"I don't know ... yet."

I was irritated. "I don't know anything you don't know."

"That may be but I'm convinced the murderer *thinks* you know something. He wants you out of the way. Now, before it's too late, tell me what you saw out there in the water."

"Nobody can say you aren't stubborn." I sighed. "I'll tell you again that I didn't see anything. I can also tell you that, since I didn't send you that note, somebody else must've ... somebody who either does know what happened or else, for reasons of his or her own, wants to implicate Brexton anyway. If I were you, I'd go after the author of that note." A trail which, I was fairly certain, would lead, for better or worse, to the vindictive Claypoole.

Greaves was deep in some theory of his own. I had no idea what it was. But he did seem concerned for my safety and I was touched. "I must warn you, Mr. Sargeant, that if you don't tell me the whole truth, everything you know, I won't be responsible for what happens."

"My unexpected death?"

"Exactly." I had the sensation of being written off. It was disagreeable.

Chapter Four

1

At midnight I arrived at the party which was taking place in a rundown gray clapboard cottage near the railroad station, some distance from the ocean. The Bohemian elements of Easthampton were assembled here: thirty men and women all more or less connected through sex and an interest in the arts.

Nobody paid any attention to me as I walked in the open front door. The only light came from stumps of candles stuck in bottles: the whole thing was quaint as hell.

In the living room somebody was playing a guitar, concert style, while everybody else sat on the floor talking, not listening. I found Liz in the dining room, helping herself to some dangerous-looking red wine.

She threw her arms about me dramatically. "I was so terrified!" I murmured soothing words to her while a bearded fat man drifted by, playing with a yo-yo.

Then she looked at me carefully and I could see, under the play acting, that she was genuinely concerned. "You're sure you feel all right?" she felt my head; her eyes growing round when she touched the bump which was now like a solid walnut.

"I feel just fine. Do you think you ought to drink that stuff?" I pointed to the wine which had come from an unlabeled gallon jug, like cider.

"I don't drink it. I just hold it. Come on, let me introduce you to the host."

The host was a burly man with an Indonesian mistress who stood two paces behind him all evening, dressed in a sari, wedgies and a pink snood. She didn't know any English which was probably just as well. Our host, a sculptor, insisted on showing me his latest work which was out in a shed at the back of the house. With a storm lantern we surveyed his masterpiece in reverent silence: it was a lump of gray rock the size of a man with little places smoothed off, here and there.

"You get the feeling of the stone?" The sculptor looked at me eagerly; I wondered if Liz had told him I was an art critic.

"Very much so. Quite a bit of stone too. Heavy."

"Exactly. You got it the first time. Not many people do. Heavy . . . the right word though you can't describe sculpture in words . . . but it's the effect I was after: heavy, like stone . . . it *is* stone."

"*Heavy* stone," I said, rallying.

He was in an ecstasy at this. "You have it. He has it, Liz. *Heavy* stone . . . I may call it that."

"I thought you were calling it the 'Dichotomy of St. Anne'?"

"Always use a subtitle. By God, but that's good: heavy stone."

In a mood of complete agreement and mutual admiration, we rejoined the party.

Liz and I joined a group of young literary men, all very sensitive and tender with sibilants like cloth tearing; they sat and gossiped knowingly about dissident writers, actors, figures all of the new decline.

While they hissed sharply at one another, Liz and I discussed my problems or, rather, the problems at the North Dunes.

I told her what I really thought about the morning's adventure. "I don't think anybody was trying to kill me. I think somebody was up to something in the house and they didn't want to be observed. They saw me coming and they were afraid I might interfere so I was knocked over the head while they made their retreat. Anybody who wanted to kill me could've done so just as easy as not."

"It's awful! I never thought I'd know somebody mixed up in anything like this. How does it feel, living in a house with a murderer?"

"Uncomfortable . . . but kind of interesting."

"You should hear the talk at the Club!"

"What's the general theory?"

"That Brexton killed his wife. Everybody now claims to've been intimate friends of theirs and knew all along something horrible would happen."

"They may have a surprise ahead of them."

"You don't think he did it, do you?"

"No, I don't think so; he must've been tempted though."

"Then what makes you think he *didn't* do it?"

"A hunch . . . and my hunches are usually wrong." I was getting tired of the whole subject. Every lead seemed to go nowhere and there weren't many leads to begin with.

We tried to figure on possible places to go later on that evening but since I was tired and not feeling particularly hearty from my blow on the head and since we were both agreed that though sand was glamorous and all that for making love on in the moonlight it was still scratchy and uncomfortable: several sensitive areas of my body were, I noticed earlier that day, a little raw, as though caressed with sandpaper, it seemed best to put off until the next night our return engagement. But though we were both fairly blithe about the whole thing, I found her even more desirable than before we'd made love which is something that seldom happens to me: usually, after the first excitement of a new body, I find myself drifting away; this time it looked as if it might be difficult. I vowed, though, that there would be no serious moments if I could help it.

Along about one o'clock somebody began to denounce T.S. Eliot and a thick blonde girl took off most of her clothes to the evident boredom of the young men who were recalling happy days on Ischia while two intense contributors to the *Partisan Review* began to belt each other verbally for derelictions which no one else could follow: it was a perfect Village party moved out to the beach.

Liz and I lay side by side on the floor, talking softly about nothing at all, everything forgotten but the moment and each other.

I was interrupted by Dick Randan. "Didn't expect to find you here," he said, looking at us curiously.

"Oh ... what?" I sat up and blinked at him stupidly. I'd been so carried away I'd lost all track of everything. He was about the last person I'd expected to see in that place. I told him as much.

He sat down on the floor beside us, a little like a crane settling on a nest. "I'm an old friend of Evans'," he said, indicating our host who was showing a sheaf of his drawings to the bearded man who'd put away his yo-yo and gone to sleep sitting bolt upright in the only armchair in the room.

"How were things back at the house?" I asked.

"All right, I guess. I left right after you did and went to the Club; there wasn't much on there so I came over here ... took a chance Evan might still be up. I handled his Boston show, you know."

Then I introduced him to Liz. They nodded gravely at each other. Across the room the half-naked blonde was sitting cross-legged like a Yogi and making her heavy white breasts move alternately. This had its desired effect. Even the sensitive young men stopped their cobra-hissing long enough to watch with wonder.

"Nothing like this will ever happen at the Ladyrock Yacht Club," I said austerely.

"I'm not so sure," said Liz, thoughtfully. "I wonder how she does that."

"Muscle control," said Randan and, to my surprise, he showed certain unmistakable signs of lust; for some reason I had automatically assigned him to the vast legions of Sodom . . . showing you never can tell.

"Somebody did something under the table once at the Club," said Liz. "But it was one of the terrace tables and there wasn't any light to speak of," she added, making it all right.

The blond ecdysiast then rose and removed the rest of her apparel and stood before us in her mother-earth splendor: she was, as they say with a leer in low fictions, a real blonde.

The Indonesian mistress then decided that this was too much; she went out of the room, returning a moment later with a large pot of water which, with an apologetic oriental smile, she poured all over the exhibitionist who began to shriek.

"It's time to go," said Liz.

A brawl had just begun, when we slipped out a side door into the moonlight. Randan came with us, still exclaiming with awe over the blonde's remarkable control. "People study for years to learn that," he said.

"It must be a great consolation on long winter evenings," I said. Then I discovered that Liz had no car tonight and, though I much preferred getting a taxi or even walking home, Randan insisted on driving us in his car.

I gave Liz a long good-night kiss at the door to her house while the collegian looked the other way. Then with all sorts of plans half-projected, she went inside and Randan drove me back to the North Dunes.

He was more interesting than I'd thought, especially about the murder which intrigued him greatly. "I've made a study of such things," he said gravely. "Once did a paper on the murder of Sir Thomas Overbury . . . fascinating case."

"Seventeenth century, wasn't it?" I can still recall a few things to confound undergraduates with.

"That's right. I hadn't planned to come down here though Allie invited me. Then, when I heard about what happened, over the radio in Boston, I came on down. I used to know Mrs. Brexton slightly ... when she was going with my uncle."

"That was quite a while ago."

"Fifteen years, I guess. I remember it clearly though. Everybody took it for granted they'd be married. I never understood why they didn't ... next thing we knew she married Brexton."

"Your uncle and aunt seem awfully devoted to each other."

But he was too shrewd to rise to that bit of bait. "Yes, they are," he said flatly.

The North Dunes was black against the white beach. It looked suddenly scary, sinister, with no lights on ... I wondered why they hadn't left a hall light for me.

We parked in the driveway. I couldn't see anybody on the darkened porch. I remembered only too well what had happened the last time I stepped into that gloomy house, late at night. "You staying here?" I asked turning to Randan.

"No, I'm in the village. I don't want to get involved; lot of other people I want to see while I'm in Easthampton." He got out of the car. "I'll walk you to the house."

I was ashamed of my own sudden fear. I hoped Randan hadn't noticed it.

We skirted the front porch and approached the house from the ocean side.

He talked all the time about the murder which didn't make me any too happy. For the first time since the trouble began, I was afraid, an icy, irrational fear. I wanted to ask him to go inside with me but I didn't have the nerve, too ashamed to admit how shaky I was. Instead, I filibustered, answering his questions at great length, putting off as long as possible my necessary entrance.

We sat down on a metal swing which stood near the steps to the porch, a little to one side of the several unfurled beach umbrellas, like black mushrooms in the night. Moonlight made the night luminous and clear.

We sat very still to keep the swing from creaking.

"I came down here," said Randan softly, "for a definite reason. I know Allie thinks I'm just morbid but there's more to it than that. I'm very fond of her and my uncle. I was worried when I heard all this had happened."

"You mean that they might be . . . involved?"

He nodded. "I don't mean directly. Just that an awful lot of stuff might come out in the papers that shouldn't . . . gossip."

"About your uncle and Mildred Brexton?"

"Mainly, yes. You see my hunch is that if they try to indict Brexton he'll drag Fletcher and Allie into the case . . . just to make trouble."

It was uncanny. These were practically the same words I had overheard between Brexton and Claypoole the day of the murder. Uncle and nephew had evidently exchanged notes . . . or else there was a family secret they all shared in common which made them nervous about what Brexton might do and say in court.

"What did you intend to do?" I asked, curious about his own role.

He shrugged. "Whatever I can. I've been awfully close to Fletcher and Allie. I guess they're more like parents to me than uncle and aunt. In fact when my father died, Fletcher became my legal guardian. So you see it's to my interest to help them out, to testify in case there's . . . well, an accusation against them."

"What sort of accusation? What is Brexton likely to pull?"

Randan chuckled. "That'd be telling. It's not anything really . . . at least as far as this business goes. Just family stuff."

I had an idea what it was: the relationship between brother and sister might be misconstrued by a desperate man; yet what had that to do with the late Mildred Brexton? Randan was no help.

He shifted the subject to the day of the murder. He wanted to know how everybody behaved, and what I thought had actually happened in the water. He was

91

keener than I'd suspected but it was soon apparent he didn't know any more than the rest of us about Mildred's strange death.

I offered him a cigarette. I took one myself. I lighted his. Then I dropped the matches. Swearing, I felt around for them in the sand at my feet.

I retrieved them at last. I lit my own cigarette. It was then that I noticed that my fingers were dark with some warm liquid.

"Jesus!" I dropped both matches and cigarette this time.

"What's the matter?"

"I don't know ... my fingers. It looks like blood. I must've cut myself."

"I'll say; you're bleeding." Randan offered me a handkerchief. "Take this. How'd you do it?"

"I don't know. I didn't feel a thing." I wiped my fingers clean only to find that there was no cut. The blood was not mine.

We looked at each other. My flesh crawled. Then we got to our feet and pushed aside the metal swing.

At our feet was a man's body, huddled in its own blood on the white sand. The head was turned away from us. The throat had been cut and the head was almost severed. I walked around to the other side and recognized the contorted features of Fletcher Claypoole in the bright moonlight.

Chapter Five

1

There was no sleep in that house until dawn.

Greaves arrived. We met by candlelight in the drawing room. It seemed that shortly after midnight the lights had gone out which explained why there'd been no light in the house when Randan and I arrived. One of the plain-clothes men had been testing the fuse box in the kitchen for over an hour, without success.

Everyone was on hand but Allie Claypoole who had caved in from hysteria. A nurse had been summoned and Allie was knocked out by a hypo . . . a relief to the rest of us for her shrieks, when she heard the news, jangled our already taut nerves.

No one had anything to say. No one spoke as we sat in the drawing room, waiting to be called to the alcove by detective Greaves. Randan and I were the only two dressed; the others were all in night clothes. Brexton sat in a faded dressing gown, one hand shielding his face from the rest of us. Mary Western Lung, looking truly frightened, sat huddled, pale and lumpy, in her pink, intricate robe. Mrs. Veering snuffled brandy with the

EDGAR BOX

grimness of someone intending to get drunk by the quickest route. Randan and I were the observers, both studying the others ... and one another for I was curious to see how he would take the death of a favorite uncle and guardian: he was the coolest of the lot. After his first shock when I thought he was going to faint, he'd become suddenly businesslike: he was the one who had the presence of mind not to touch the body nor the long sharp knife which lay beside it, gleaming in the moon. He had called the police while I just dithered around for a few minutes, getting used to the idea of Fletcher Claypoole with his head half off.

The women were called first; then Randan; then me ... Brexton was to be last, I saw. For the first time I began to think he might be the murderer.

It was dawn when I joined Greaves in the alcove. The others had gone to bed. Only Brexton was left in the drawing room. The lights were now on. Greaves looked as tired and gray as I felt.

I told him everything that had happened. How Randan and I had talked for almost twenty minutes before discovering the body beneath the swing.

"What time did you arrive at the house of ..." he consulted his notes gloomily, "Evan Evans?"

"A few minutes before twelve."

"There are witnesses to this of course."

"Certainly."

"What time did Mr. Randan arrive at this house?"

"About one fifteen, I'd say. I don't know. It's hard to keep track of time at a party. We left at one thirty, though. I remember looking at my watch." I was positive he was going to ask me why I looked at my watch but he didn't showing that he realized such things can happen without significance.

"Then you dropped off Miss Bessemer and came straight here?"

"That' right?"

"At what time did you find the body?"

"One forty-six. Both Randan and I checked on that."

94

Greaves strangled a yawn. "Didn't touch anything, either of you?"

"Nothing ... or maybe I did when I got blood on my fingers, before I knew what was under the swing."

"What were you doing out there? Why did you happen to sit down on that swing?"

"Well, we'd just come home from the party and there weren't any lights on in the house and Randan wanted to talk to me about the murder of Mrs. Brexton so we walked around the house and sat down here. I suppose if a light'd been on we'd have gone inside." I didn't want to confess I'd been scared to death of going into that house alone.

"Didn't notice anything odd, did you? No footprints or anything?"

"Nothing. Why were the lights out?"

"We don't know. Something wrong with the master fuse. One of our men was fixing it while the other stood guard." Greaves sounded defensive. I could see why.

"And the murder took place at twelve forty-five?"

"How do you know that?" He snapped the question at me, his sleep-heavy eyes opening suddenly wide.

"It fits. Murderer tampers with fuse box; then slips outside, kills Claypoole in the swing while the police and others are busy with the lights; then ..."

"Then what?"

"Well, then I don't know," I ended lamely. "Do you?"

"That's our business."

"When did the murder take place?"

"None of your ..." but for reasons best known to himself, Greaves paused and became reasonable: I was the press as well as a witness and suspect. "The coroner hasn't made his final report. His guess, though, was that it happened shortly after the lights went out."

"Where's the fuse box?"

"Just inside the kitchen door."

"Was a policeman on guard there?"

"The whole house is patrolled. But that time there was no one in the kitchen."

95

"And the door was locked?"

"The door was unlocked."

"Isn't that odd? I thought all cooks were mortally afraid of prowlers."

"The door was locked after the help finished washing up around eleven. We have no idea yet who unlocked it."

"Fingerprints?"

Greaves only shrugged wearily.

"Any new suspects?"

"No statement, Mr. Sargeant." He looked at me coldly.

"I have a perfect alibi. I'm trustworthy." I looked at him with what I thought were great ingenuous spaniel eyes. He was not moved.

"Perfect alibis are dirt cheap around here," said the policeman bitterly.

2

I found out the next morning what he meant.

I awakened at eight thirty from a short but sound sleep. I spent the next half hour scribbling a story for the *Globe* . . . eyewitness stuff which I telephoned to the city desk, aware that I was being tuned in on by several heavy breathers. Then I went downstairs to breakfast.

Through the front hall window I caught a glimpse of several newspapermen and photographers arguing pathetically with a plain-clothes man on the porch . . . I had, I decided a pretty good deal, all in all . . . if I stayed alive of course. The possibility that one of the guests was a homicidal maniac had already occurred to me; in which case I was as fair a victim as anyone else. I decided the time had come to set my own investigation rolling . . . the only question was where?

In the dining room a twitchy butler served me eggs and toast. Only Randan was also down. He was radiant with excitement. "They asked me to stay over, the police asked me, so I spent the night in my uncle's room."

"Wasn't that disagreeable?"

"You mean Allie?" His face became suddenly gloomy. "Yes, it was pretty awful. But of course the nurse stayed with her all night, knocking her out, I guess, pretty regularly. I didn't hear anything much even though the walls around here are like paper. It was also kind of awful being in Fletcher's bed like that . . . luckily, the police took all his things away with them."

"You see anybody yet this morning?"

He shook his head, his mouth full of toast. "Nobody around except the police and the reporters out front. They certainly got here fast."

"It'll be in the afternoon papers," I said wisely. "Have they found out anything yet about the way he was killed?"

"Don't know. I couldn't get much out of Greaves. As a matter of fact he got sore when I asked him some questions . . . said one amateur detective was enough for any murder case. Wonder who he meant?"

" 'Whom' he meant," I said thoughtfully, aware that Harvard's recent graduates were not as firmly grounded in *English Usage* as my generation. "I expect he meant me."

"You're not a private detective, are you?" He looked at me fascinatedly, his eyes gleaming behind their thick lenses.

"No, but I'm an ex-newspaperman and I've been mixed up in a couple of things like this. Nothing quite so crazy, though."

"Crazy? I've got a hunch it's perfectly simple."

"Well, that's good to hear. Why keep us in suspense any longer?" My sarcasm was heavy; I am not at my best at breakfast.

"Maybe I won't." He looked mysteriously into his coffee cup. I found him as irritating as ever. He was my personal choice for murderer with Mary Western Lung a close second.

"I suppose you think Brexton did it because he's jealous and wanted to kill not only his wife but her lover too, selecting a week end at his wife's aunt's house as the correct setting for a grisly tableau?"

"I don't see what's wrong with that theory ... even if you do try to make it sound silly. There's such a thing as spur-of-the-moment murder, isn't there? And this was the first chance he had of getting them both together." Randan was complacent.

"Why wasn't he cleverer about it? I know most painters are subaverage in intelligence but if he wanted to get away with these murders he couldn't have picked a worse way of going about it."

"Well, I'm not saying I think he did it. I'll make you a bet, though: that I figure this out before either you or Greaves." I told him I'd take him up on that: twenty dollars even money.

The morning was sunny and cool outdoors; the sea sparkled; the police were everywhere and Greaves, it developed, had moved over from Riverhead and was now staying in the house, in Brexton's downstairs room (the painter was assigned a room upstairs) and we were all told to stay close to the premises for the rest of the day.

I set to work on the alibis.

Both Mrs. Veering and Miss Lung, it developed, had gone to bed at the same time, about twelve thirty, leaving Allie and Brexton together in the drawing room. Randan was at the club. Claypoole took his last walk at midnight. None of the ladies had, as far as I could tell, an alibi. Allie of course was still knocked out and no one had been able to talk to her. I was beginning to wonder what Greaves had meant by perfect alibis being cheap. I discovered after lunch.

Brexton was treated like a leper at lunch. Everyone was keyed up, and frightened. It was easy for me to get him away from the others.

"Let's take a walk," I said. We were standing together on the porch overlooking the ocean.

"I wonder if they'll let us . . . or me," said the painter.

"We can try." We strolled out the door, pausing a moment on the terrace. New sand had been raked over the dark blood beneath the swing. The seat was calm. No visible sign of death anywhere to mar the day.

We walked, a little self-consciously, past the swing and down onto the sand. A plain-clothes man appeared quietly on the terrace, watching us. "I feel very important," Brexton smiled dimly. "We'd better not walk far."

In plain view of the detective, we sat down on the dunes a few yards from the house. "You're a newspaperman, aren't you?" Brexton was direct.

"Not exactly. But I'm writing about this for the *Globe.*"

"And you'd like to know how I happened to drown my wife and murder an old family friend on a quiet week end at the beach? That would be telling," he chuckled grimly.

"Maybe something short of a confession then," I said, playing along.

"Do you really think I did it?" This was unexpected.

I was honest. "I don't know. I don't think so, for a number of reasons that would be of no use to you in court."

"My own approach exactly."

"Who do *you* think did it?"

He looked away. With one hand he traced a woman's torso in the sand: I couldn't help but watch the ease with which he drew, even without watching the lines . . . not at all like his abstractions. "I don't think I'll say," he said, finally. "It's only a hunch. The whole thing's as puzzling to me as it is to everybody else . . . more so since most of them are quite sure I did it. I'll tell you one thing: I couldn't have committed either murder."

This had its desired effect. I looked at him with some surprise. "You mean. . . ."

"Last night when Claypoole was killed, assuming it

happened before one fifteen, just before your arrival on the beach with Randan, I was with Allie Claypoole."

This of course was the big news; the reason for Greave's gloom early that morning. "You told the police this?"

"With some pleasure."

"And they believed you?"

"All they have to do is ask Allie."

"But she's been hysterical or unconscious ever since, hasn't she?"

He frowned slightly. "So they say. But when she's herself again they'll find out that there was no way on earth I, or Allie for that matter, could have killed her brother."

We were both silent. I recalled as closely as I could everything which had happened the night before: had there been any sound when Randan and I circled the house? Any marks upon the sand? All I could see in my mind though was that great dark house in the wild moonlight. Dark! I thought I'd found a hole in his story.

"If you were talking to Miss Claypoole how come you were in the dark? There wasn't a light on in the house when we got there."

"We were on the porch, in the moonlight."

"The porch overlooking the terrace?"

"No, on the south side, the golf course side."

"I wonder where the police were."

"One patrolled the house regularly, while the other was looking for extra fuses which the butler had mislaid. The policeman had flashlights," he added, "to round out the picture."

"Picture of what is the question."

"Picture of a murderer," said Brexton softly and with one finger he stabbed the torso of the figure in the sand. I winced involuntarily.

"Is there anything you'd like me to say?" I asked, trying to make myself sound more useful than, in fact, I was. "I'll be doing another piece tomorrow and . . ."

"You might make the point that not only was I with

100

Miss Claypoole when her brother was killed but that my wife was in the habit of taking large quantities of sleeping pills at any time of the day or night and that four was an average dose if she was nervous. I've tried to tell the police this but they find it inconvenient to believe. Perhaps now they'll take me seriously."

"Mrs. Brexton was not murdered? She took the pills herself?"

"Exactly. If I know her, her death was as big a surprise to her as it was to the rest of us."

"You don't think she might have wanted to kill herself? to swim out where she knew she'd drown."

"Kill herself? She planned to live forever! She was that kind." But he wouldn't elaborate and soon we went back to the house while the plain-clothes man watched us from the shadow of the porch.

That afternoon Liz paid a call and we strolled along the beach together to the Club; apparently the policeman didn't much care what I did.

Liz was lovely and mahogany-dark in a two-piece affair which wasn't quite a bathing suit but showed nearly as much. I was able to forget my troubles for several minutes at a time while watching her scuff along the sand, her long legs were slender and smooth with red paint flaking off the toenails as she kicked shells and dead starfish.

But she wouldn't let me forget the murders for one minute. She had read my piece in the *Globe* which was just out, and all the other papers too. "I don't think it's safe," she said after she'd breathlessly recited to me all the bloody details she'd read that afternoon.

"I don't think so either, Liz, but what can I do?" I was willing to milk this for all it was worth ... the thought that she might be erotically excited by danger to the male (cf. behavior of human females in wartime) was appealing, but not precise. Liz, I think, has no imagination at all, just the usual female suspicion that everything's going to work out for the worst if some woman doesn't step in and restore the status to its pre-

101

vious quo. There wasn't much room for her to step in, though, except to advise.

"Just leave, that's all you have to do. They can't stop you. The worst they can do is make you appear at the trial, to testify." The dramatic possibilities of this seemed to appeal to her; her knowledge of the technicalities were somewhat vague but she was wonderful when she was excited, her eyes glowing and her cheeks a warm pink beneath her tan.

I maneuvered her into the dunes just before we got to the Club. She was so busy planning my getaway that she didn't know until too late that we were hidden from view by three dunes which, though they didn't resemble the mountains of Idaho did resemble three pointed smooth breasts arranged in a warm triangle. She started to protest; then she just shut her eyes and we made love, rocking in the cradle of white hot sand, the sky a blue weight over our heads.

We lay for a while together, breathing fast, our hearts in unison quieting. I was relaxed for the first time in two tense days. Everything seemed unimportant except ourselves. But then the practical Liz was sitting up, arranging her two-piece garment which I'd badly mangled in a bit of caveman play.

I waited for some vibrant word of love. Liz spoke: "You know, darling, there are such things as beds, old-fashioned as that may sound."

It served me right, I decided, for expecting the familiar thick honey of love. "I bet it doesn't scratch you as much as it does me," I said, pulling up my old G.I. slacks, aware that sand had collected in private places.

"You know so little about women," said Liz kindly. "I'll get you a chart and show you how our anatomy differs from the male who is based on a fairly simple, even vulgar plumbing arrangement."

"I suppose the female is just dandy."

"Dandy? Magnificent! We are the universe in symbol. The real McCoy. Gate to reality, to life itself. All men envy us for being able to bear children. Instead of walking around with all those exterior pipes, we ... ."

"Sexual chauvinism," I said and rolled her back onto the sand but we did not make love this time. We just lay together for a while until the heat became unbearable; then both wringing wet, we ran to the club a few yards down the beach.

The Ladyrock, by day, is a nautical-looking place with banners flying, a pool where children splash around, a terrace with awning for serious drinkers, rows of lockers and cabanas, a model Club on a model coast and full of model members, if not the pillars, at least the larger nails of the national community.

I was a little nervous about being introduced to Liz's aunt who sat with a group of plump middle-aged ladies in pastel-flowered dresses and wide hats, all drinking tea under a striped umbrella. I was sure that our lust marked us in scarlet letters but, outside of the fact that on a fairly cool day we were both flushed and dripping sweat, there was apparently no remarkable sign of our recent felicities. Liz's aunt said we were both too old to be running races on the sand and we were dismissed.

"Races she calls it!" I was amused as I followed Liz to her family's cabana.

"I'm sure that's what she thinks sex is anyway." Liz was blithe. "They had no sense of sport in those days." I don't know why but I was shocked by this. I realized from hearsay that, although Liz was occasionally willing, she was far from being a sexual gymnast like so many girls of her generation. The real rub of course was to hear her talk the way I usually did. I resented her lack of romance, of all the usual messiness which characterizes even the most advanced modern lovers. I wondered if she was trying deliberately to pique me; if she was, she was succeeding. I was willing to do almost anything to get a rise out of her: just one soulful look, one sigh, one murmured: "I wish this could go on forever," would have made me feel at home. Instead, she was acting like a jaded high school boy in his senior summer.

We washed up carefully in the shower of the cabana and then I put on a pair of her uncle's trunks which hung sadly from my pelvis, to her delight. "I wish all men would wear them like that," she said, pouring herelf into a bright green creation which fitted her like scales do a snake. "Leaves more to the imagination." And then she was off in a lightning break for the ocean. I didn't overtake her until she was well into the first line of breakers.

We weren't back on the beach until the cocktail crowd had arrived. Hundreds of brightly dressed men and women were gathering beneath the umbrellas. They formed in separate groups like drops of oil in a glass of water. Certain groups did not speak to others. Those with too much money were treated as disdainfully as those with too little. Even here in paradise you could tell the cherubim from the seraphim.

Liz's aunt belonged to the top-drawer-but-one old guard: a group of middle-aged ladies who played bridge together, deplored the wicked influences which each year gained ground in the village, whispered about the depravities and bad taste of those richer than they, smiled tolerantly at the nervous carefulness of those poorer and, in general, had themselves a good time while their husbands, purple of face, slow of mind, wheezed about golf scores in the bar.

Liz spared me her aunt and we found ourselves a vacant table close to the pool where we drank a newly invented cocktail, the work of the club bartender who was obviously some kind of genius: gin, white mint, mint leaves, a dash of soda. I looked forward to getting drunk. The sun was warm, though late. The salt dried with a delicate tickle on my skin. Liz was beside me . . . everything was perfect except Dick Randan who joined us, wearing a jazzy pair of plaid trunks which set off the sallowness of his skin, the millions of visible sharp bones in his skinny body.

"Playing hooky, I see," he said with a boom of heartiness in imitation of the old bucks at the bar. Uninvited, he sat down.

"How are you today, Miss Bessemer?" He turned his spectacles in her direction. I wanted to kick him.

"Fine, thank you," and Liz gave him her best Vivien-Leigh-as-Scarlet-O'Hara smile.

"I suppose you heard about what happened to us last night after we left you."

"Yes," said Liz softly and she fluttered her eyelids shyly; she was giving him the business and I almost burst out laughing. Randan fell deeply.

"It's been a terrible strain," he said tensely, flexing one minuscule bicep.

"You must have nerves of absolute steel!" Liz trilled.

"Well, not exactly but I guess Pete here has told you a little what it's like."

"I should crack up in five minutes," said that girl of stone with an adoring glance at both of us.

"It's not easy," said Randan with lips heroically thinned. I intervened. "Was I missed at the house?"

"No, the guard saw you coming over here with Miss Bessemer."

"Oh?" I waited to hear more of what the guard saw but evidently he was a man of discretion. Randan went on: "So I thought I'd come over and see who was around. I was getting a bit tired of that atmosphere. You know Allie is still knocked out, don't you?"

"I thought she was up by now."

Randan shook his head. "No, she's been raving, in an awful state. Nobody's allowed near her except Greaves. I finally went to him . . . you know, as next of kin, and demanded a report on her condition. He told me she hadn't made sense since early this morning. I told him her place was in a hospital but he said she was under expert medical care, whatever that is around here."

Liz stopped her teasing at last, enthralled as usual by our situation. "Do you think they'll really arrest Mr. Brexton?" she asked.

Randan shrugged. "It's hard to say. Some of us aren't entirely sure he's responsible," he added weightily.

"Oh, but it *has* to be Mr. Brexton."

"Why is that?" I was surprised by her confidence.

"Because only a man could have cut Mr. Claypoole's throat. Peter hadn't any reason to do that, so that leaves just Brexton."

"And me," said Randan, nodding. "I'm a suspect too."

"Oh, but you were out that night; besides you wouldn't kill your uncle ... anyway even if you could've there was no way for you to kill Mrs. Brexton since you were in Boston. . . ."

"Spending the day with friends," added Randan stuffily. "Don't think I didn't have to prove to Greaves that I was up there when it happened."

"So then you have two alibis, which rules you out. Only poor Mr. Brexton could've done both murders."

"Very neat," I said. "But suppose 'poor Mr. Brexton' has an alibi for the second murder and a good explanation for the first?"

"What's that?" They both looked at me curiously.

"I have no intention of telling either of you anything until you read it tomorrow in the *Globe*. But I will say that I happen to know Brexton was with Allie Claypoole at the time of the murder."

Randan looked at me with some interest. "Are you sure of this?"

"Certainly. And I think it rules him out."

"Unless . . ." Liz paused. We both looked at her, a little embarrassed by the sudden consequences of what I'd said.

"Unless what?" Randan's voice was edgy.

"Unless, well, they did it together ... which might explain why she went to pieces afterwards." This fell cold and unexpected between us.

"Miss Claypoole is my aunt ..." began Randan dryly.

Liz cut him short with luminous apologies. "I didn't mean anything, really. I was just talking. I don't know anything about anything; just what I've read and been told. I wouldn't for the world suggest that she or anyone . . ." Liz brought the scene to a polite end. But we left her, after another round of drinks, with the definite sensation that something shocking had happened, that some strange vista had been unexpectedly opened.

We were halfway down the beach to the house before either of us spoke. It was Randan who broke the silence. "I can't believe it," he said finally.

"About your aunt and Brexton? Well, it was just one of Liz's more hairbrained theories."

"But the damned thing is it might make sense to that fool Greaves; I couldn't let that happen."

"I'm sure it won't occur to him."

"Won't occur to him? What else will occur to him when he hears they were together? It leaves only three other possibilities: myself, Miss Lung and Mrs. Veering. I wasn't around and I don't think the two ladies have any motive. Brexton was trying to bluff you."

I nodded. "I've taken that into account. It's more than possible."

Randan shook his head worriedly. "But that doesn't make sense because when Allie recovers she'll deny his story . . . if he's made it up."

I was soothing. "There's probably more to the murder than we know. Maybe he was killed before the time supposed. Maybe Brexton zipped out of the house, murdered him and then came back in again, all under the pretext of going to the bathroom."

"Too complicated." But his face brightened as he considered these complexities. "Anyway we've got to look after Allie now. I'm going to suggest they put an extra guard on duty just to look after her."

"Why?"

"Well, if he was bluffing he won't want her to come to, will he?" The logic was chilling, and unarguable.

We found Greaves standing in his crumpled gray business suit along on the terrace, studying the swing.

"How's my aunt?" asked Randan.

"Where the hell you been?" Greaves looked at him irritably. "I wanted to talk to you."

"I went over to the Club. Is she . . ."

"Still the same."

"What did you want to ask me?"

"We'll go into that after dinner."

Randan then demanded a full-time guard for Allie which was refused on the grounds that two plain-clothes men in the house and a full-time nurse was quite enough. When Greaves demanded to know why protection was needed, Randan clammed up, then, with a look at me to implore silence, he went into the house to change for dinner.

Something occurred to me just as I was about to go inside myself. "I was wondering," I said, "why you haven't asked me any more questions about that note you found, the one you thought I'd manufactured for your amusement."

"You said you didn't, so that's that." But this fell flat.

"You think you know who fixed it, don't you?"

"That's possible."

"The murderer?"

Greaves shook his head. "Claypoole," he said.

I was more surprised by his admission than by his choice. "Why? Did you find fingerprints or something?"

"Just plain horse sense," Greaves was confident. "Claypoole suspected all along Brexton was the murderer. He didn't dare come out in the open and accuse him because of family connections, scandals, things which would affect him too. So he sent the note to give us a clue. Unfortunately, it gave Brexton a clue too and he was able to kill Claypoole before he could tell us the inside story of what went on between the three of them, or maybe even the four of them. A story which we're unraveling pretty fast right now."

This left me breathless to say the least. "You realize you're accusing Brexton of murder?"

"That's right." Greaves was almost frivolous. I wondered what new evidence the police had unearthed. Greaves enlightened me. "It seems that Claypoole was first knocked unconscious; then he was dragged up to the terrace where his throat was cut."

"How do you know he was dragged? Were there any marks on the sand?"

"Sand in his clothes. The tracks, if there were any, got rubbed out by the tide."

I didn't follow his reasoning. "Why do you think this implicates Brexton?"

Greaves only smiled.

I thought of something. "If Claypoole was first knocked unconscious, it means that a woman could've done it, doesn't it? Isn't that what a woman would do? And since she wasn't strong enough to carry him, she'd be forced to drag the body up to the terrace where she'd then cut his throat with . . . with . . ."

"A knife belonging to Brexton. A knife covered with his fingerprints." Greaves looked at me slyly, his case nearly done.

Chapter Six

1

I'm quite sure now that Greaves was bluffing. He suspected Brexton was the murderer and he had enough
circumstantial evidence to turn the whole thing over to
the District Attorney's office but he knew that many
a good minion of the law has hung himself with circumstantial evidence which a bright defense has then
used to embarrass the prosecution. Greaves had no
intention of moving for an indictment which would not
stick. His bluff to me was transparent: he wanted to
create in everyone's mind a certainty of Brexton's
guilt; if this could be done, the case would certainly be
strengthened psychologically . . . and Greaves, I'd discovered, was a devoted if incompetent amateur psy-
chologist.

I went up to my room and took a long bath, recon-
structing the revelations of the day. There had been a
number and none seemed to fit the picture which was
slowly beginning to form in my mind.

I had tracked down most of the alibis. Anyone could
have put sleeping pills in Mildred Brexton's coffee ex-

cept Randan who was in Boston that day. The two Claypooles and Brexton knew where the sleeping pills were located. Miss Lung could not have known. Mrs. Veering might have known since she was undoubtedly one of those hostesses who enjoy snooping around their guests' possessions.

Alibis for the second murder were all somewhat hazy, excepting Allie's and Brexton's; if they had really been together at the time of the murder, it either ruled them both out as murderers, or worse, ruled them in as joint killers for reasons unknown ... at least in her case. Mrs. Veering had no alibi nor did Miss Lung. Randan did; he was at the Club. Who then, logically, was in the best position, motive aside, to have committed both murders, allowing of course that all alibis were truthful?

The answer was appalling but inevitable: Mrs. Veering.

I dropped the soap and spent several minutes chasing it around the bathtub while my mind began to adjust to this possibility.

Of all the suspects she alone had no alibi for either murder ... other than a possible claim of ignorance as to the whereabouts of the various bottles of sleeping pills. If Brexton and Allie were not joint murderers, then the only person left who might have killed both Mildred and Claypoole was Mrs. Veering who, as far as I knew, had no motive.

The thought of motives depressed me. The "how" of any murder is usually a good deal simpler than the "why." These people were all strangers to me and I had no way of knowing what tensions existed between them, what grievances were hidden from the outside world. But at least Greaves and I were in the same boat. He didn't know any more than I did about the people involved. He had the advantage though of a direct mind: Brexton was quarreling with his wife. Brexton killed his wife. Claypoole threatens to expose him out of his love for the dead woman. Brexton kills Claypoole, using his own knife which he thoughtfully leaves beside the body to amuse the police.

At that point, I ruled Brexton out. He hadn't done the murder. I had a hunch, though, that if anyone knew who had done it, he did. Meanwhile, there was the problem of motives to sort out and Mrs. Veering was now my primary target. She would be a slippery customer since, even at best, she didn't make much sense.

I was just pulling on my trousers when Mary Western Lung threw the door between our two rooms open and stood before me, eyes burning with lust and bosom heaving. I realized too late that the bureau which I had placed between our connecting door had been moved to its original position by some meddling servant.

With great dignity I zipped my fly. "You were looking for me, Miss Lung?"

She pretended embarrassment and surprise, her eagle eyes not missing a trick. "I don't know what I'm doing, honestly!" She moved purposefully forward. I pulled my jacket on and shoved a chair between us, all in one dazzling play.

"Sit down, Miss Lung."

"My friends call me Mary Western," she said, sinking disappointedly into the chair. "I was so immersed in 'Book-Chat' that, when I finished, instead of going out of the door to the hall I just barged." She gave a wild squeak which was disconcerting . . . it was obviously intended to reproduce a ripple of gay laughter at her own madcap derringdo: it was awful.

I mumbled something about the perils of authorship.

"But of course *you* would understand. By the way I read with great interest your account of our tragedies in the *Globe*. I had no idea you were a past master of the *telling* phrase."

"Thanks." I tied my tie.

"But I think you should have consulted some of us before you went ahead. There are wheels within wheels, Mr. Sargeant."

"I'm sure of that."

"Yes, wheels within wheels," she repeated relishing her own telling phrase.

Then she got to the point. "I must tell you that I do not altogether agree with your diagnosis of the case."

"Diagnosis?"

She nodded. "It was perfectly clear from your piece in the *Globe* ... between the lines, that is ... that you feel Brexton did not kill either his wife or Fletcher...."

"And you feel he did?"

"I didn't say that." She was quick, surprisingly so. "But, in the light of what evidence there is, I don't see any basis for your confidence."

"I'm hardly confident ... anyway, it was, as you say, between the lines."

"Perfectly true but I thought I should talk to you about it if only because you might, without meaning to of course, make trouble for the rest of us."

"I don't ..."

"I mean, Mr. Sargeant, that if Brexton did not do the murders then one of us must have ... it's perfectly simple."

"That's logical. I had even thought that far ahead myself."

She was impervious to irony. "And if it is one of us, we are all apt to be dragged *very deep* into an unpleasant investigation which might seriously affect us all, personally and professionally. You follow me?"

I said that I did. I also said that I could hardly see what the famous author of "Book-Chat" had to fear from an investigation.

"No more perhaps than the rest of us who are innocent ... and no less." She was mysterious. She was also plainly uneasy.

"I'm afraid we're all in for it anyway," I said, sounding practical. "I don't think my reporting makes much difference one way or another. We're all in for some rough questioning ... that is if Brexton doesn't confess or something dramatic happens."

"Why make it worse? I'm convinced he killed Mildred. . . ."

"You weren't originally."

"Only because I couldn't believe that such a thing had happened, *could* happen. Now my only hope is to see this thing quickly ended and Brexton brought to justice. He was tempted . . . God knows: *I* know. Mildred had not been herself for a year. She was becoming simply impossible. The night before she died she got hysterical . . . at darling Rose, of all people, and attacked her with a knife . . . the very same knife Brexton used to kill Fletcher. Oh, it was terrible! Her attacking Rose I mean. Rose screamed: it woke us all up, remember? And then of course Brexton came rushing in and stopped . . ."

I was now listening with, I must confess, my mouth open with surprise. I didn't want to arrest her incoherent flow for fear she might clam up; at the same time I knew that what she was saying was extremely important.

When she paused for breath, I asked with affected calm, "That's right, Mildred and Mrs. Veering stayed in the drawing room after we went up to bed, didn't they?"

"Why yes . . . that's when the quarrel started. Rose told me about it later. Brexton had gone to bed and I suppose Rose was scolding Mildred about her behavior when Mildred just lost her head and rushed at her with a knife . . . poor darling! Rose was *out of her mind* with terror. She screamed and Brexton came rushing in and slapped Mildred. It was the only thing to do when she was in one of her passions. Then he took her off to bed and Rose came upstairs, telling us not to worry . . . you remember that."

"I wonder how Mildred happened to have the knife . . . it's a kind of palette knife, isn't it . . . in the drawing room?"

Miss Lung shrugged. "With a madwoman, you never know. Rose of course was positive Mildred wanted to

115

kill her. She has been like that for years about many
people and we've always humored her ... I mean you
know how Rose is: impulsive, and of course her little
vice doesn't make for one hundred per-cent rationality,
does it? But it seems that this time Rose was right and
Mildred did attack her. . . ."

"Why?"

"That is none of our business," said Miss Lung
coldly. "But I *will* say that they were great friends *before* her breakdown. Rose was loyal to her afterwards
when many people didn't want to have her around. She
even invited them here for the week end so that Mildred might have a chance to relax and get a grip on
herself. Then of course the girl attacks her. It's hardly
fair. My point is that things like that are no one's business but Rose's ... they shouldn't be written about by
gossip columnists, especially since I'm convinced the
whole terrible thing is really very simple. I only hope
the police act quickly before . . ."

"Before another incident? Another murder?"

She looked almost frightened. "No, I didn't mean
that exactly." But she wouldn't go on. "I hope we're
not too late for dinner." She made a production out of
studying the heart-shaped gold watch she wore on a
chain over her heart. Then, talking "Book-Chat," we
went downstairs and joined the other guests.

Greaves sat in the center of the sofa, looking like an
unsuccessful experiment in taxidermy. He had changed
to a blue serge suit which smelled of mothballs and was
strewn with lint like snow upon a midnight clear. He
was being a member of the party tonight, not a policeman and he was, figuratively speaking, watching every
fork. The others played along as though he were an old
friend. No mention was made of the murders. The conversation was forced but general. Brexton was in excellent form which, considering the fact his head was well
in the noose, was surprising. I wondered if he was sav-
ing up a surprise or two.

I found out one significant bit of news right off; Mrs.

Veering, over the martini tray, said: "Poor Allie is still unconscious. I'm sick with worry about her."

"Hasn't she come to at all?"

"Oh yes, regularly . . . it's only the dope which keeps her out. You see, when she comes to, she starts to rave! It's simply horrible. We're so helpless . . . there's nothing anyone can do except pray."

"Have you seen her?"

"No, they won't let anybody in except the doctor, and the nurse. I have demanded a consultation and I think perhaps they'll have to have one. Mr. Randan's agreed of course as the next of kin."

"Consultation?"

"To see what's wrong with her."

"You mean . . ."

"She may have lost her reason." And on that cheerful note, we went in to dinner.

I remember looking about the table that night with some care. The odds were that the murderer was among us, quietly eating stewed tomatoes and lobster Newburg. But which one? Brexton was the calmest, no doubt banking heavily on that perfect alibi: if he was telling the truth, and we'd soon know from Allie Claypoole herself, he would be safe . . . unless of course the business was even more bizarre than any of us suspected and the two of them, like the Macbeths, had together done in her beloved brother for reasons too lurid for the family trade.

Just as the dessert was brought in, Mrs. Veering, with a strange bland smile, got to her feet and pitched head forward onto the table.

There was a stunned silence. Her tumbler landed on the thick carpet with a hollow sound. Flowers from the centerplace scattered everywhere.

Miss Lung shrieked: a thin pale noise like a frightened lovebird.

The rest of us sat frozen in our chairs while Greaves leaped from his chair and pulled her chair back from the table. "Don't anybody move," he said.

117

2

But this was not the crisis he or anyone had antici-pated. The butler came rushing in with digitalis and Mrs. Veering recovered sufficiently to say, with a ghast-ly parody of her social smile, "I'll be all right . . . heart . . . bed."

She was carried upstairs and the trained nurse un-dressed her while Greaves ordered a doctor.

Our ever diminishing party then sat rigidly about the drawing room, drinking brandy and waiting for Greaves who, with one of his plain-clothes men, was investigating Mrs. Veering's glass, her food, the table, the servants.

Miss Lung was the most affected. I was afraid she might have a stroke herself. "Poor Rose! Knew it would . . . told her . . . never listens . . . the strain, the awful strain . . . can't be helped . . . everything pos-sible, always, from the very beginning . . . alcohol . . ."

Greaves joined us within the hour. He seemed genu-inely puzzled. "Mrs. Veering is all right, we're happy to report. She has a cardiac condition, a chronic one. She had an attack and . . ."

"Drugged!" Miss Lung looked at him, her eyes wide and glassy. "I *know* she was drugged . . . like poor Mil-dred, or worse: poison!"

This is what we had all been thinking.

Greaves, without hesitation, went to the table where the whisky was kept and, regulations or no regulations, poured himself a stiff drink.

Then he joined our tense circle. "She was not drugged and she was not poisoned. She is resting comfortably. Her doctor is with her now. She may have to stay in bed a day or two but that's all."

There was nothing for us to say. Miss Lung obvi-ously did not believe him. The rest of us didn't know what to think. "No one can see her until tomorrow,"

118

said Greaves just as Miss Lung got purposefully to her feet.

"Rose is my oldest friend and when she is in her hour of need I must go to her, *come what may.*" The authoress of *Little Biddy Bit* looked every yard a heroine.

"I'm sorry but I can't allow it." Greaves was firm. Miss Lung sat down heavily, her face lowering with anger. Greaves looked at the rest of us thoughtfully.

"This is going to be a difficult night," he said. "I will tell you right off that we're waiting for Miss Claypoole to recover and give us her story of what happened the night of her brother's murder. Until we have her testimony, we can do nothing but wait."

Awkward silence greeted his candor. Everyone knew what he meant. No one said anything: no one dared look at Brexton who sat doodling with a pencil on a sketch pad. I half expected him to say something out of line but he ignored Greaves.

"Meanwhile," said Greaves with an attempt at heartiness, "you can do anything you like. We'd prefer for you to stay here but we can't force you, exactly. Should you want to go out, please check with me or with one of the men on duty. I know all this is unusual procedure but we're in an unusual situation without much precedent to go on. It is my hope, however, that we will be able to call a special court by Friday."

"What is a special court?" asked Brexton, not raising his eyes from the sketch pad on his knees.

"It's a court consisting of the local magistrate and a local jury before whom our district attorney will present an indictment of a party or parties as yet unknown for the crime of murder in the first degree." He gathered strength from the legal jargon. It was properly chilling.

Then, having made his effect, he announced that if anyone needed him he could be found in the downstairs bedroom; he went off to bed.

I went over and sat down beside Brexton, feeling

sorry for him ... also curious to find out what it was that made him seem so confident.

He put the book down. "Quiet week end, isn't it?" This wasn't in the best of taste but it was exactly what I'd been thinking, too.

"Only four left," I said, nodding. "In the war we would've said it was a jinx company."

"I'm sure it is too. But actually it's six surviving, not four, which isn't bad for a tough engagement."

"Depends how you reckon casualties. Has Mrs. Veering had heart attacks before? Like this?"

"Yes. This is the third one I know of. She just turns blue and they give her some medicine; then she's perfectly all right in a matter of minutes."

"Minutes? But she seemed really knocked out. The doctor said she'll have to stay in bed a day or two."

Brexton smiled. "Greaves *said* the doctor said she'd have to stay in bed."

This sank in, bit by bit. "Then she ... well, she's all right now?"

"I shouldn't be surprised."

"But why the bluff? Why wouldn't Greaves let anybody go to her? Why would he say she'd be in bed a few days?"

"Something of a mystery, isn't it?"

"Doesn't make any sense."

Brexton sighed. "Maybe it does. Anyway, for some reason, she wants to play possum ... so let her."

"It's also possible that she might have had a worse attack than usual, isn't it?"

"Anything is possible with Rose." If he was deliberately trying to arouse my curiosity he couldn't have been more effective.

"Tell me, Mr. Brexton," I spoke quietly, disarmingly, "who killed your wife?"

"No one."

"Are you sure of this?"

"Quite sure."

"Then by the same reasoning, Claypoole hit himself

120

on the head, dragged his own body through the sand and cut his own head off with your palette knife."

Brexton chuckled. "Stranger things have happened."

"Like what?"

"Like your knocking yourself out the other morning in the kitchen."

"And what about that? That I know wasn't self-inflicted."

Brexton only smiled.

"Your wife killed herself?"

"By accident, yes."

"Claypoole . . ."

"Was murdered."

"Do you know who did it?"

"*I* didn't."

"But do you know who did?"

Brexton shrugged. "I have some ideas."

"And you won't pass them on?"

"Not yet."

I felt as if we were playing twenty questions. From across the room came the high squeal of Miss Lung appreciatively applauding some remark of our young historian.

I tried a frontal attack. "You realize what the police will think if Allie Claypoole testifies that she was, as you say, with you when her brother died?"

"What will they think?" His face was expressionless.

"That perhaps the two of you together killed him."

He looked at me coolly. "Why would they think that? She was devoted to him. Look at the way this thing hit her. The poor child went out of her head when they told her."

"They might say her breakdown was due to having killed her own brother."

"They might, but why?"

"They still think you killed your wife. They think Claypoole had something on you. They think you killed him. If Allie says you were with her then they'll immediately think she was involved too."

"Logically but not likely. Even allowing the rest was

121

true, which it isn't, why would she help me kill her brother?"

I fired in the dark. "Because she was in love with you."

Brexton's gaze flickered. He lowered his eyes. His hands closed tight on the book in his lap. "You go too far, Mr. Sargeant."

"I'm involved in this too," I said, astonished at my luck: by accident I had hit on something no one apparently knew. "I'd like to know where we stand, that's all."

"None of your business," he snapped, suddenly flushed, his eyes dangerously bright. "Allie isn't involved in any of this. There'll be hell to pay if anybody tries to get her mixed up in it . . . that goes for the police who are just as liable to court action as anyone."

"For libel?"

"For libel. This even goes for newspapermen, Mr. Sargeant."

"I had no intention of writing anything about it. But I may have to . . . I mean, if Greaves should start operating along those lines. He's worried; the press is getting mean. He's going to have to find somebody to indict in the next few days."

"He has somebody."

"You mean you?"

"Yes. I don't mind in the least. But there won't be a conviction. I'll promise you that." He was grim.

I couldn't get him to elaborate; I tried another tack. "If neither you nor Allie killed Claypoole, that leaves only three suspects . . . Miss Lung, Mrs. Veering and Randan. Why would any of those three have wanted to kill Claypoole?"

Brexton looked at me, amusement in his eyes. "I have no intention of giving the game away, even if I could, which is doubtful. I'm almost as much in the dark as you and the police. I'll give you one lead though," he lowered his voice. "Crime of passion."

"What do you mean?"

With one quick gesture of his powerful right hand he

indicated Miss Lung. "She was in love and she was spurned, as they say."

"In love with whom?"

"Fletcher Claypoole, and for many years."

"I thought she was in love with the whole male sex."

"That too. But years ago when I first met her, about the same time Fletcher did, she was a good-looking woman. This is hard to believe, I know, but she was. All the fat came later when Fletcher wouldn't have her. I painted her once, when she was thin . . . it was when I was still doing portraits. She was quite lovely in a pale blonde way. I painted her nude."

I could hardly believe it. "If she was so pretty and so much in love with him why didn't he fall for her?"

"He . . . he just didn't." The pause was significant. I thought I knew what he didn't want to say. "But she's been in love with him ever since. I think they quarreled our first day here."

"About that?"

"About something."

"I can't see her committing murder fifteen years after being turned down."

"Your imagination is your own problem," said Brexton. He got to his feet. "I'm going to bed," and with a nod to the two on the couch, he left the drawing room.

This was the cue for all of us. Randan asked me if I wanted to go to the Club with him. I said no, that I was tired. Miss Lung waited to be invited to the Club herself but, when the invitation did not come, she said she would have to get back to her authorial labors . . . the readers of "Book-Chat" demanded her all.

I went upstairs with her. On the second floor landing one of the plain-clothes men was seated, staring absently into space. Miss Lung bade us both good night cheerily and, with a long lingering look at the servant of the public, she oozed into her room, no doubt disappointed that his services did not include amatory dalliance with Mary Western Lung.

I went to my own room and quickly shoved the bu-

123

reau against the connecting door. Then I telephoned
Liz, only to find she was out.

I went over and looked out the window gloomily and
thought of Liz, wondering whether or not I should join
Randan, who was just that moment getting into his car,
and make the round of the clubs. I decided not to. I
had an idea there might be something doing in the next
few hours, something I didn't want to miss out on.

Fully clothed, I lay down on my bed and turned the
light out. I thought about what Brexton had told me,
about what he *hadn't* told me. Very neatly, he'd provided Miss Lung with a motive. Not so neatly, he'd allowed me to discover what would, no doubt, be an important piece of evidence for the prosecution: that Allie
Claypoole and he were in love, that the two of them, as
easily as not, could've killed her brother for any number of reasons, all ascertainable.

3

I awakened with a start.

I had gone to sleep and not moved once which explained why my neck ached and my whole body felt as
though I'd just finished a particularly tough set of calis-
thenics. I don't know what awakened me. I won't say
premonition . . . on the other hand a stiff neck sounds
prosaic.

The first thing I did was to look at my watch, to see
how long I'd slept: it was exactly midnight according
to the luminous dial.

I switched on the light beside my bed and sat up,
more tired than when I'd dropped off to sleep.

I had half expected a call from Liz. The fact I
hadn't received one bothered me a little. I found I was
thinking altogether too much about her.

Suddenly the thought of a stiff shot of brandy occurred to me, like a mirage to a dying man in the Gobi.

124

I had to have one. It was just the thing to put me back to sleep.

I opened the door and stepped out into the dimly lit hall. At the far end, the plain-clothes man sat, staring dreamily at nothing. He shook his head vigorously when he saw me, just to show he was awake.

"Just going to get something," I said cheerfully.

He grunted as I passed him. I went downstairs. The lights were still on in the drawing room. I remember this surprised me.

I had just poured myself some brandy when Miss Lung, pale and flurried, arrayed in her pink awning, materialized in the doorway.

"Where is the nurse? Have you seen the nurse?"

"What nurse?" I looked at her stupidly.

"The nurse who. . . ."

"Someone looking for me?" A brisk female voice sounded from the main hall. Miss Lung turned as the nurse, white-clad and competent, appeared with a covered tray.

"Yes, I was. A few minutes ago I went into Rose's room to see how she was . . . I know that nobody's allowed to do that but I just didn't care. Anyway, she wasn't in her bed. I rapped on Allie's door and there wasn't any answer there either and I was afraid. . . ."

"I'm the night nurse," said the white figure. "We change at midnight. I was in the kitchen getting a few things ready. As for Miss Claypoole she is under morphine and wouldn't be able to hear you. . . ."

"But Rose? Where on earth can she be?"

"We'll find out soon enough." We made an odd procession going up those stairs. The angular angel of mercy, the billowy plump authoress of "Book-Chat," and myself with a balloon glass of brandy in one hand.

The guard stirred himself at the sight of this procession. "I told her she wasn't supposed to go in there but. . . ."

Miss Lung interrupted him curtly. "This is Mrs. Veering's house, my good man, not the city jail."

We went into Mrs. Veering's room first and found

our hostess, handsome in black lace, sitting up in bed reading a detective story. She was dead sober for once and not at all like her usual self. She was precise, even formidable.

"What on earth is everybody doing . . ." she began but Miss Lung didn't let her finish.

"Oh, Rose, thank heavens! I was terrified something had happened to you. I was in here a few minutes ago and you were nowhere in sight; then I rapped on Allie's door." She indicated the connecting door, "and there wasn't any answer. I couldn't've been more terrified!"

"I was in the bathroom," said Mrs. Veering, an unpleasant edge to her voice. "I'm perfectly all right, Mary. Now do go to bed and we'll have a nice chat tomorrow. I still feel shaky after my attack."

"Of course I will, Rose, but before I go you must . . ." while the two women were talking, the nurse had opened the connecting door and gone into Allie's room. She had left the door half open and I maneuvered myself into a position where I could look in. I was curious to see how Allie looked.

I saw all right.

The nurse was already on the telephone. "Doctor? Come quickly. An injection. I don't know what. I think she'll need an ambulance."

Before the law intervened to keep us all out, I was at Allie's bedside.

She lay on her back, breathing heavily, her face gray and her hands twitching at the coverlet. The nurse was frantically examining a hypodermic needle.

"What happened?"

"Someone's given her an injection." The nurse managed to pump a last drop of fluid from the hypodermic on a piece of cotton. "It's . . . oh God, it's strychnine!"

126

4

This time the questioning was general. There were no private trips to the alcove.

Greaves joined us an hour to the dot after the ambulance took Allie to the hospital.

Mrs. Veering was on hand, pale and hard-eyed, her own attack forgotten in the confusion. Miss Lung was near hysteria, laughing and giggling uncontrollably from time to time. Brexton was jittery. He sat biting his knuckles, his old faded dressing gown pulled up around his ears, as though to hide his face. Randan, who'd arrived during the confusion, sat with a bewildered look on his face while Greaves explained to us what had happened.

"She'll be all right," were his first words. He paused to see how the company responded: relief in every face . . . yet one was acting. Which?

Greaves went on, not looking at anyone in particular. "Somebody, at midnight exactly, got into Miss Claypoole's room and attempted to give her an injection of strychnine. Luckily whoever did this did a sloppy job. Very little was introduced into the artery, which saved her life." He pulled out a tablet of legal-size paper.

"Now I'm going to ask each of you, in order, to describe where he or she was at midnight. Before I start, I should say for those who are newcomers to this house that on the second floor there are seven bedrooms, each with its own bath. The hall runs down the center of the floor with a window at either end. On the west side is the staircase and three bedrooms. On the north, farthest from the stairs, is Mr. Sargeant's room. Next to him is Miss Lung. Next to her is an empty room and south of that of course is the stairs. Three bedrooms and a stairwell on the west side." He paused a moment; then: "All contiguous bedrooms open into one another, by connecting doors in the rooms themselves . . . *not* through the bathrooms which do not connect."

"I can't see what all this had to do with what's happened," said Mrs. Veering irritably.

"It has a great deal . . . as I hope to show you in a few minutes." Greaves made some marks none of us could see on the tablet. "Now, on the other side of the hall, the east side overlooking the ocean, there are four bedrooms. The north bedroom belongs to Mr. Randan. The next to Mrs. Veering. The next to Miss Claypoole and the last to Mr. Brexton. Both Mr. Brexton and Mrs. Veering are in bedrooms which have doors which open into Miss Claypoole's room."

"The door in my room is locked," said Brexton suddenly. His voice made us all start.

"That's correct," said Greaves quietly. "It was locked this morning by me, from Miss Claypoole's side of the door. The key was not in the lock, however."

"What do you mean by that?" Brexton's voice was hard.

"All in good time. And don't interrupt, please. Now I hope you will all be absolutely honest. For your own safety."

There was a grave silence. Greaves turned to me. "Where were you at midnight?"

"In bed, or maybe just waking up."

"Do you always sleep fully dressed?"

"Not always. I just dozed off. I hadn't intended to go to sleep but I did, probably around eleven or so."

"I see. And you say you woke up at twelve."

"That's right. I looked at my watch. I was surprised I'd been asleep. I turned on the light and decided that a drink of brandy might be just the thing to get me back to sleep."

"And you went downstairs?"

"As you know." I was aware that, while I talked, Greaves was recording everything in shorthand; this was an unexpected talent. I described to him what had happened.

He then turned to Miss Lung. "We'll move from

room to room, in order," he said. "Yours is next. Where were you at midnight?"

"I ... I was in Rose's ... in Mrs. Veering's room, looking for her."

"Are you sure it was midnight?"

"No, not exactly but I guess it must've been because I was only in there a few minutes and I saw Mr. Sargeant right afterwards. I was *terrified* when I didn't find her. Then, when I knocked on Allie's door and got no answer, I knew something *must* be wrong; I rushed off to find the nurse. The policeman on duty saw me."

"Unfortunately, he didn't see you go in. He *did* see you come out. He was standing on the top stair, it seems, talking to the nurse going off duty, his back to the hall when you went into Mrs. Veering's room, at ten minutes to twelve."

"I ... I was only in there a *very* few minutes."

"Yet the nurse went off duty at ten minutes to, or rather left Mrs. Veering's room at that time to meet her relief who was arriving downstairs. She paused to chat with the man on duty. While this was happening, you went across the hall from your room to Mrs. Veering's, isn't that right?"

"Well, yes. I did notice the policeman was talking to somebody on the stair. I couldn't see who it was. . . ."

"Miss Lung, did you try to open the door between the two rooms?" There was a tense silence. Miss Lung was white as a sheet. Brexton sat on the edge of his chair. Mrs. Veering's eyes were shut, as though to blot out some terrible sight.

"I. . . ."

"Miss Lung did you or did you not try to open that door?"

The dam broke. The cord of silence snapped. Miss Lung wept a monsoon. In the midst of her blubberings, we learned that she *had* tried to open the door and that it was locked, from the other side.

It took several minutes to quiet Miss Lung. When she was at last subdued, Greaves moved implacably on.

"Mr. Randan, will you tell me where you were at midnight?"

Reluctantly, Randan tore his gaze from the heaving mound which was Mary Western Lung. "I was in my room."

"What time did you come back to the house?"

"I don't know. Quarter to twelve or so. The night nurse and I arrived at the same time. We came in the house together. We both went upstairs; she met the other nurse who was on duty and I went to my room. I was just about to get undressed, when the commotion started."

"When were you aware of any commotion?"

"Well, I thought something was up even before I heard anything definite. I heard Sargeant's door open and close. It's right opposite mine so I could tell he was up. Then I heard somebody stirring next door to me . . . it must've been Miss Lung. I didn't pay much attention until I heard them all running up the stairs."

"What did you do then?"

"I went out in the hall and asked the man on duty what was happening. He said he didn't know. Then you appeared and. . . ."

"All right." Greaves turned to Mrs. Veering. "And where were *you* at. . . ."

"I was sitting on the toilet." The crude reply was like an electric shock. Miss Lung giggled hysterically.

"You were there from ten minutes to twelve until twelve o'clock?"

"I don't carry a stop watch, Mr. Greaves. I was there until I finished and then I went back to bed. The next thing I knew, three maniacs were in my room." This was a fairly apt description of our invasion.

"Did you see or hear anything unusual during those ten minutes?"

"No, I didn't."

Evidently Greaves hadn't been prepared for such prompt negatives. He started to ask her another question; then he decided not to. She was looking dangerously angry. I wondered why.

Greaves turned to Brexton and put the same question to him he had to the rest of us.

"At twelve o'clock I was sound asleep."

"What time did you go to bed?"

"I don't know. Eleven . . . something like that."

"You heard nothing unusual from the next room, from Miss Claypoole's room?"

"Nothing in particular."

"Then what in general?"

"Well . . . moving around, that's about all. That's before I went to sleep."

"And when you awakened?"

"It was around midnight: I thought I heard something."

"Something like people running? Or shutting doors?"

"No, it was a groan . . . or maybe just my imagination or maybe even the noise of the surf. I don't know. It's what awakened me though. Then of course everybody started to rush around and I got up."

"This sound that you heard, where did it come from?"

"From Allie's room. I thought it was her voice too. I think now maybe it was."

"What did you do when you heard it?"

"I . . . well, I sat up. You see there was only a few seconds interval between that and everyone coming upstairs."

Greaves nodded; his face expressionless. "That's very interesting, Mr. Brexton. You didn't by any chance try to open the door did you? The door between your room and Miss Claypoole's?"

"No, I knew it was locked."

"How did you know that?"

"Well, I . . . I tried it some time ago . . . the way you do with doors."

"The way *you* do, Mr. Brexton."

"It's a perfectly natural thing to do." Brexton flushed.

"I'm sure, especially under the circumstances." Greaves reached into his pocket and pulled out a handkerchief which he unwrapped. It contained a key which he was careful not to touch. "What is this, Mr. Brexton?"

"A key."

"Have you ever seen it before?"

"How do I know! All keys look alike."

"This is the key to the door which leads from your room to Miss Claypoole's."

"So what?"

"It was found twenty minutes ago, hidden in the pillowcase of your bed. Mr. Brexton, I arrest you on suspicion of an attempted murder in the first degree. You may inform your attorney that a Special Court will be convened this Friday in Easthampton. I am empowered by the State of New York. . . ."

Miss Lung fainted.

Chapter Seven

1

Brexton was arrested and taken to jail at two A.M. Tuesday morning. The Special Court was scheduled for Friday. This gave me two days to track down the actual murderer for the greater glory of self and the blind lady with the scales. Forty-eight hours in which I was apt as not to find that Brexton was indeed the killer.

I got up the next morning at nine o'clock. I was barely dressed when the managing editor of the *Globe* was on the phone.

"Listen, you son of a bloodhound, what d'you mean by slanting those damned stories to make it sound like this Brexton wasn't the murderer?"

"Because I don't think he is." I held the receiver off at arm's length while my one-time employer and occasional source of revenue raved on. When the instrument quieted down, I put it to my ear just in time to hear him say, "I'm sending Elmer out there to look into this. He's been aching to cover it but no, I said, we got Sargeant there: you remember Sargeant? bright-eyed,

wet-eared Sargeant, I said, he'll tell us all about it he'll
solve the god-damned case and what if the police do
think Brexton killed his wife Sargeant knows best, I
tell him, he'll work this thing out. Ha! You got us out on
a sawed-off limb. Elmer's going to get us off."

"Flattery will get you nowhere," I said austerely.
"Neither will Elmer. Anyway what would you say if I
got you the real murderer, exclusively, and by Friday?"

"Why don't you. . . ."

I told him his suggestion was impractical. Then I
told him what he could do with Elmer, if he was in the
mood. I hung up first.

This was discouraging, Elmer Bush, author of the
syndicated column, "America's New York" which, on
television, became the popular weekly resumé of news
"New York's America" was my oldest rival and enemy.
He had been a renowned columnist when I was only
assistant drama editor on the *Globe*. But, later, our
paths had crossed and I had managed twice to get the
beat on him news-wise, as we say. This was going to be
a real trial, I decided gloomily.

I called Liz who sounded wide-awake even though I
was positive she'd only just opened her eyes.

"They arrested Brexton last night."

"No!" She made my eardrum vibrate. "Then you
were wrong. *I* thought he did it. Of course that's just
woman's intuition but even so it means *something*.
Look at all the mediums."

"Medium what's?"

"The people who talk to the dead . . . they're almost
always women."

"Well, I wish you'd put in a call to Mildred Brexton
and. . . ."

"Oh, don't tease. Isn't it exciting! Can I come over?"

"No, but I'll see you this afternoon if it's all right."

"Perfect. I'll be at the Club after lunch."

"What happened to you last night?"

"Oh, I was at the Wilson's dance. I was going to call
you but Dick said you'd gone to bed early."

"Randan? Was he there?"

134

"Oh yes. He's sweet, you know. I don't know why you don't like him. He was only there for a while but we had a nice chat about everything. He wanted to take me up to Montauk for a moonlight ride in his car but I thought that was going too far. . . ."

"I'm glad you have limits."

"Don't be stuffy." After a few more cheery remarks, I hung up. This was apparently going to be one of those days, I decided. Elmer Bush was arriving. Randan was closing in on Liz. Brexton was in jail and my own theories were temporarily discredited.

Whistling a dirge, I went down to breakfast.

The sight of Randan eating heartily didn't make me feel any better. No one else was down. "See the papers?" He was beaming with excitement. "Made the front pages too."

He pushed a pile toward me. All the late editions had got the story "Painter Arrested for Murder of Wife and Friend" was the mildest headline. By the time they finished with the relationships, it sounded like something out Sodom by way of Gomorrah.

I didn't do more than glance at the stories. From my own newspaper experience I've learned that newspaper stories, outside of the heads and the first paragraph, are nothing but words more or less hopelessly arranged.

"Very interesting," I said, confining myself to dry toast and coffee . . . just plain masochism. I enjoyed making the day worse than it already was.

"I guess neither one of us got it," said Randan, ignoring my gloom. "I suppose the obvious one is usually the right one but I could've sworn Brexton didn't do it."

"You always thought he did, didn't you?"

Randan smiled a superior smile. "That was to mislead you while I made *my* case against the real murderer, or what I thought was the real murderer. But I didn't get anywhere."

"Neither did I."

"That business of the key clinched it, I suppose," said Randan with a sigh, picking up the *Daily News*

135

which proclaimed: "Famous Cubist Indicted: Murders Wife, Cubes Friend."

I only grunted. I had my own ideas about the key. I don't like neatness. I also respect the intelligence of others, even abstract painters: Brexton would not have left that key in his pillow any more than he would have left his palette knife beside the body of Claypoole. In my conversations with him he had struck me as being not only intelligent but careful. He would not have made either mistake if he'd been the killer.

I kept all this to myself. Accepting without comment Randan's assumption (and everybody else's) that justice was done and murder had out.

Mrs. Veering and Miss Lung came down to breakfast together. Both seemed controlled and brisk.

"Ah, the gentlemen are up with the birds!" exclaimed the penwoman brightly, fully recovered from her dramatic collapse of some hours before.

"I'm afraid it's been something of an ordeal, Peter." Mrs. Veering smiled at me. She was pale but her movements were steady. Apparently she had, if only briefly, gone on the wagon: she was quite a different person sober than half-lit.

I mumbled something inane about: well, things could've been worse.

"And I'm afraid we won't be able to carry through our original project either."

I had already given it up but I pretended to be thoughtful, a bit disappointed. "Yes, I think you're right under the circumstances," I said, nodding gravely. "It might not be the wise thing to do. . . ."

"I knew you'd understand. I'm only sorry you've wasted nearly a week like this. . . ."

"Not *all* wasted."

She smiled. "That's right. You got several stories out of it, didn't you?"

Miss Lung chimed in. "Thrillingly presented, Mr. Sargeant! I can't wait to see what your account of the *murderer at bay* will be like."

"Tense," I said, "very tense."

"I can hardly wait! Though Heaven knows any reminders of what we've just gone through will be unpleasant, to say the least. Rose, we have been tested, all of us, in the furnace of experience."

"And emerged bloodied but unbowed," said Mrs. Veering who could scramble a saw with the best of them. I asked to be excused, pleading work.

"Certainly." Mrs. Veering was amiable. "By the way, Mr. Graves or whatever his name is, called me this morning to say he'd like us all to stay together, in Easthampton, that is, until after the Special Court. I hope it won't inconvenience you; you're welcome to stay here of course till then."

I said that was fine by me.

I went to my room and telephoned my secretary, Miss Flynn.

"The Case has broken Wide Open," she said in the tone of one who follows crime at a careful distance.

"Looks like it." I had no intention of saying anything over that phone which would give anyone listening in an idea of my private doubts. "I'll be back Friday afternoon. Any news?"

She gave me a precise summary of what had happened in my absence. I told her what should be done for the various clients. I then asked her to check a few things for me.

Though they sounded odd she was, as usual, reticent; she made no comment.

"I shall, as you know, exert every effort to comply with these Requests," she said formally. "Incidentally, a Mr. Wheen has been calling you every day. Has he attempted to Contact you yet?"

I said no and she said he hadn't stated his business so that was that.

My next move, after hanging up, was strategic.

In the room next to me, Miss Lung's, I could hear a mild vacuuming. The entire second floor was empty, except for the one maid. Stealthily, I left my own room, crossed the hall, and entered Dick Randan's room.

It was a fair duplicate of my own. He hadn't both-ered to unpack and his suitcase lay open and full of rumpled clothes. I went through everything quickly. Aside from the fact that he wore Argyle socks with large holes in them, there was nothing unusual to be found. I was looking for nothing in particular, which naturally made my search all the more difficult. I *did* want to get the layout of the rooms clear in my mind though.

I cased the bathroom and found the usual shaving things: I also found a woman's handkerchief with the initials R.V. It was wadded up and stuck in a glass on the second shelf of the medicine cabinet. R.V. was Rose Veering but why Randan had her handkerchief in his bathroom was a mystery. It was unmarked ... no blood stains or anything interesting, just a lace-type handkerchief, as they say in bargain basements. Puz-zled, I put it back. Could he be a kleptomaniac? Or a fetishist? Or had Mrs. Veering made love to him in the night, leaving this handkerchief as a token of her affec-tion? Or had he just happened to find it and picked it up and stuffed it in the nearest receptacle which was, in this case, a drinking glass? I decided I was going out of my mind, ascribing significance to everything.

I went back into his bedroom and looked at the two windows, both of which were open. Being a corner room he had two views: one of the dunes to the north with a half glimpse of beach, the other of the terrace directly below and the umbrellas; the sea was calm, I saw. On this side, directly beneath the window, the roof of the first-floor porch sloped. The window screens, I noticed, were the permanent, all-year-round kind.

Then I opened the door between Randan's room and the next bedroom, Mrs. Veering's. This was the largest of all the rooms with three windows overlooking the ocean. It was expensively furnished, very pink and silken and lacy. It was also full of bric-a-brac, clothes ... too much stuff to do more than glance at.

I did find something fairly interesting in her bathroom. On a metal table was a small autoclave on

138

which was placed several hypodermic needles and vials of medicine, all neatly labeled with her name and the contents. Two of the vials contained strychnine which, I knew vaguely, was the stuff to be given a failing heart in an emergency. Obviously Mrs. Veering was prepared for anything. . . .

The door to what had been Allie Claypoole's room was unlocked. It smelled like a hospital. Her clothes were still there, all neatly arranged in the closet and in the drawers of the bureau. If there was anything remotely like a clue the police had doubtless found it by now. I skimmed hurriedly through everything and then went on to Brexton's room. It was a mess with the mattress on the floor and the sheet and pillows scattered around on the floor. Someone had come for his clothes apparently; and there was no longer any sign of his residence. I found nothing . . . except that the window to his room, the window which looked east on the ocean, was directly above the metal swing beneath which I'd found the body of Fletcher Claypoole. Since there had been a full moon that night, Brexton *could* have seen the murderer if he had looked out that window . . . his view was the only one from the second floor which allowed an unobstructed view of the swing; the others had their view of it blocked by umbrellas and awnings.

Not much to go on but still a possibility . . . and it might explain Brexton's seeming confidence: he had actually witnessed the murder of Claypoole. Yet, if he had, why had he kept silent? It was a puzzle. I had no idea the solution was already at hand.

2

I waited around until eleven thirty for Greaves to show up but it developed that he was about the state's business in Riverhead, and wallowing in a sea of official approbation. The legal machinery was now being set in motion by the District Attorney's office and the doughty Greaves could rest on his laurels.

When I was sure that he wasn't going to pay us a visit, I asked Randan if I could borrow his car. He was gracious about it, only asking me if I was sure I had a driver's license. I said I was and I took the car.

The day was crisp and clear, more autumn than summer. Along the main street of Easthampton the elms had begun to yellow a bit at the edges. Winter was near.

I drove straight to the Hospital of St. Agatha where I knew Allie Claypoole had been taken.

With an air of confidence which I didn't feel, I walked into the gloomy Victorian brick building, told the receptionist that I was Dick Randan, Miss Claypoole's nephew, and that I wanted very much to see her.

To my surprise, after a few minutes of whispering into telephones, I was told that I could see her, for ten minutes but that I must not in any way excite her. She had been, it developed, conscious and collected for some hours.

She lay propped up in a hospital bed, her face white as paper but her eyes clear and bright. She was completely rational. She was startled to see me. "I thought Dick . . ." she began.

I interrupted her quickly. "Wanted to come but sent me instead. I wondered if I could talk to you alone." I glanced at the nurse who was fumbling efficiently with various sedatives on a tray.

"Against doctor's orders. *And* police's orders," said the nurse firmly. "Don't worry; I won't listen."

Allie smiled wanly. "I'm afraid we'll have to obey orders. Why do you want to see me, Mr. Sargeant?"

I sat down close to her bedside, pitching my voice low.

"I wanted to see how you were, for one thing."

"Nearly recovered. It seems the strychnine, instead of killing me, provided just the jolt I needed. They tell me I was in some danger of losing my mind." She said

140

all this matter-of-factly. She was in complete control of herself.

"You don't remember anything? I mean about the strychnine. . . ."

She shook her head. "I didn't come to until the ambulance."

"You were with Brexton when your brother was killed?"

She nodded. "I've already told the police that, this morning when that awful little man came to see me."

"They didn't want to believe you, did they?"

"No, they didn't. I can't think why."

"Did you know they've arrested Brexton?"

Her eyes grew wide; she skipped a breath; then she exhaled slowly and shut her eyes. "I should have known," she whispered. "No, they didn't tell me but that explains why they seemed to be disappointed when I told them. I think they wanted to cross-question me but the doctor told them to go. Paul *couldn't* have done it. He had no reason to do it. He was with me."

"We haven't much time," I spoke rapidly. "I don't think Brexton did it either but the police do and they've got a good deal of evidence, or what they think is evidence. Now you must help me. I think this thing can be solved but I've got to know more about the people involved, about past history. Please tell me the truth. If you do, I think we can get the charges against Brexton dismissed."

"What do you want to know?"

"Who had any reason to kill your brother?"

She looked away. "It's hard to say. I mean, what exactly is *enough* reason. There are people who have grievances but that doesn't mean they would kill. . . ."

"Like Miss Lung?"

"Well, yes, like her. How did you know about that?"

"Never mind. What actually happened between her and your brother?"

"Nothing. That was the trouble. She was in love with him. He was not in love with her. We all lived in Boston then, as you know. We saw a great deal of each other. I suppose you know she wasn't fat in those days ... she was rather good-looking. It nearly killed her when he took up with Mildred. About that time she began to get fat ... I don't think it was glandular, just neurotic reaction. She never went with another man, as far as I know, and she never stopped loving Fletcher...."

"Could she have drugged Mildred do you think?"

"I ... I've wondered that all along. She hated Mildred. I think she hated Mildred even more when she turned down Fletcher ... one of those crazy things: hates her for being a rival and then hates her even more for rejecting the man she herself loves. Yes, I think she might've drugged Mildred but it seems odd she should wait fifteen years to do it."

"Perhaps this was her first opportunity in all that time."

"Perhaps. I don't know. Even if she did, why would she then kill Fletcher?"

"Revenge? For his having turned her down."

"I wonder. At first I thought it was an accident, that Mildred had just taken an overdose of pills and gone in swimming but then, when the police got involved, why, it occurred to me that Mary Western Lung gave Mildred those sleeping pills if only because no one else there really hated poor Mildred ..."

"Not even her husband?"

Allie shrugged. "He was used to her. Besides, he had plenty of better opportunities: he wouldn't pick a week-end party to kill his wife."

"You disliked Mildred, didn't you?"

"She was not a friend of mine. I disliked the way she tried to hold on to Fletcher after she'd married Brexton. We quarreled whenever we met, usually about my keeping him in Cambridge when she thought he should live in New York where she could get her claws into him."

"*Did* you keep him in Cambridge?"

She smiled sadly. "There was no keeping him anywhere except where he wanted to be. He was never interested in Mildred after she married. In fact, she bored the life out of him."

"Yet she went right on . . . flirting with him."

"If that's the word. She was possessive certainly."

"Would your brother have wanted her dead?"

Allie looked at me with startled eyes. "What do you mean?"

"I'm just trying to cover all the motives, that's all. I wondered if for any reason he might've had a motive."

"I can't think why. Of course not. You don't kill old girl friends just because they bore you."

"I suppose not. Now for your nephew. Would he have had any reason to want to kill Mildred?"

She shook her head. "I don't think he ever met her more than once or twice. Besides, he was in Boston. I happened to talk to him the night before she died, long distance."

"Family business?"

"In a way. I also invited him to come down here. Rose had said it would be all right."

"Then that rules him out as far as Mildred goes. Did he have any reason to want your brother dead?"

She shook her head, slowly. "No, not really. They weren't very sympathetic. Two different types. Fletcher was his guardian you know. I don't think they ever openly quarreled though last winter there was some kind of flare-up, over money. Fletcher controls Dick's estate and Dick wanted to get it all in his own name. But Fletcher was firm and that was the end of that. They've seen very little of each other since."

"Then I gather Randan wasn't eager to come down here."

She smiled. "He refused when I telephoned him. He was nice about it but I could tell he didn't want to see Fletcher. I thought he should . . . I'm the peacemaker, you know."

"I suppose curiosity about Mildred brought him?"

She nodded. "He's fascinated with crime."

I had to work fast. "And Mrs. Veering?" Across the room I could already see the nurse growing restive.

143

"We met her about the same time we met Mildred ... we had mutual friends. Rose and I have always been close; Rose was more upset than anyone when Mildred didn't marry Fletcher."

"Would she have any motive, do you think? For either murder?"

Allie shook her head. "None that I know of. Mildred was a trial but then she didn't have to see her if she didn't want to. For the last year, she hadn't wanted to ... I was surprised when Rose asked us down and told us the Brextons would also be in the house. I thought she'd stopped seeing her. It seemed odd ... Fletcher and I weren't sure we wanted to come. Oh, God, how I wish we hadn't!" This was the first sign of emotion she'd displayed during our talk. The nurse looked disapprovingly at me. Allie bit her lower lip.

I was relentless; there was little time. "Mrs. Veering was friendly with your brother?"

"Of course. No, there's no motive there. I can't think of any possible reason for Rose to want to . . ."

"Then you'd rule her out altogether as the murderer?"

Allie only shook her head, confusedly. "I don't know what to think. It's all so horrible."

The nurse said. "Time for you to go, sir."

I asked my last question. "Are you in love with Brexton?"

She flushed at this. "No, I'm not."

"Is he with you?"

"I . . . you'd better ask him, Mr. Sargeant."

3

I found Liz on the terrace of the Club guzzling contentedly in the company of several distinguished members of the international set, including Alma the Marchioness of Edderdale, a raddled, bewildered creature with dark blue hair who had inherited a Chicago meat fortune with which she'd bought a string of husbands among whom the most glamorous had been the late Marquess. She wandered sadly about the world, from center to center, set to set, in a manner reminiscent of a homing pigeon brought up in a trailer.

She looked at me with vague eyes when we were introduced: I've known her for years. "Charmed," she sighed, her face milk-pale beneath the wide hat she wore to protect herself from the sun. On her arms elbow-length gloves, circled at the wrist by emeralds, hid the signs of age. Her face had been lifted so many times that she now resembles an early Sung Chinese idol.

Liz quickly pulled me away. She was delighted with the news. "It's all just as I said, isn't it?" Only the fact she looked wonderful in red kept me from shoving her face in.

"Just as you said, dear."

"Well, aren't you glad? You're out of that awful house and the thing's finished."

"I'm holding up as well as possible."

"Oh, you're just being professional! Forget about it. People make mistakes. Everybody makes mistakes. I read your pieces in the *Globe* faithfully . . . of course it was perfectly clear you thought Brexton didn't do it but I'm sure the *Globe* won't be mad at a little thing like that. I mean, look at Truman that time."

"Truman who? At what time?"

"Truman the President the time when he got elected and they said he couldn't. Nobody minded everybody being wrong."

I maintained her innocence. Heads had fallen that dark year. One head might fall this year. Of course I could live without the *Globe,* but even so an old alliance would be forever gone if I didn't dish up something sensational.

At that moment my nemesis, Elmer Bush, wearing canary yellow slacks, a maroon sports jacket, alligator shoes and a smile such as only the millions who watch him on television ever get from his usually flint-like face, moved resolutely toward me, hand outstretched, booming, "Long time no see, Brother Sargeant!"

I forced down a wave of nausea and introduced him

to the table; everyone seemed more pleased than not to have this celebrated apparition among them.

"Quite a little to-do you been having in these parts," said the columnist, slapping me on the back in the hopes I had a sunburn. I didn't. I punched his arm fraternally, a quick judo-type rabbit punch calculated to paralyze the nerves for some seconds. But either he was made of foam rubber or I've lost the old magic. He didn't bat an eye.

"*Globe* felt I ought to come down for a look-see."

"A what?" I still kept my old buddy smile as a possible cover-up for another friendly jab in his arm (I'd figured I'd missed by an inch the nerve center) but he moved out of range.

"A look-around ... always the kidder, Pete. Ha! Ha! Been reading those pieces you wrote. Some mighty good on-the-spot coverage, if I say so myself."

"Thanks." I waited for the blow to fall: it did.

"Of course you backed the wrong horse. Got them sort of peeved at the city desk. You know how sensitive they are. Course I never figure anything you say in the papers makes a damned bit of difference since everybody's forgot it by the next edition but you can't tell an editor that." This was the columnist's credo, I knew. I had often wondered how Elmer had avoided a lynching party: his column is in many ways the dirtiest around town ... which puts it well into the province of the Department of Sanitation, Sewer Division.

"He hasn't been indicted yet."

"Friday." Elmer smacked his lips. "Had a little chat with Greaves ... old friend of mine. Used to know him when I covered Suffolk County in the old days." This was probably a lie. Elmer, like all newsmen, tends to claim intimacy with everyone from Presidents to police officials. "He's got a good little old case. That key! man, that's first-class police work."

I groaned to myself. Liz, I saw, was enchanted by the famous columnist. She listened to him with her pretty mouth faintly ajar. I said wearily: "You're right, Elmer. It takes real cunning to search a man's room and find a key. They don't make policemen nowadays like they used to in Greaves' day."

Elmer sensed irony ... something he doesn't come in contact with much in his line of snooping in the wake of elopements and divorces and vice-raids. "Don't sell Greaves short," he said slowly, his face solemn, his manner ponderous. "There aren't too many like him around ·... clear-headed thinkers. That's what I like about him. You could've picked up a lot from him. I did. I'm not ashamed to admit it ... I'll learn from any man." There was a pause as we all considered this.

Then I asked gravely, innocently, "You also find out why Brexton used the key to get into Miss Claypoole's room?"

Bush looked at me as though I'd gone off my head. "You been in publicity too long," he said at last, contemptuously.

"He stole the key from Mrs. Veering ... it was kept in her desk, by the way, right in the top drawer where anybody could've swiped it ... and he unlocked Miss Claypoole's door when he heard the nurse go off duty. Then he tiptoed in, took a hypodermic, filled it with strychnine, tried to give her a shot, failed ... ran back to his room and locked the door, hiding the key in his pillowcase."

"Oh, isn't that fascinating!" Treacherous Liz was carried away with excitement.

"The strychnine," I said quietly, "was kept in Mrs. Veering's room, not in Miss Claypoole's. How could he've got it?"

"Any time ... any time at all." Elmer was expansive.

"Perhaps. That leaves only one other mystery. I'm sure you and Greaves have it worked out though: *why* did Brexton want to kill Allie?"

"Keep her from testifying."

"Yet she has already testified that she was with Brexton at the time her brother was killed, isn't that right? Well, it doesn't make sense, his trying to destroy his only alibi."

Elmer only smiled. "I'm not at liberty to divulge the prosecution's case . . . yet."

I was appalled at the implications. Neither Elmer nor Greaves was a complete fool. Did this mean that the state was going to try to prove that Allie and Brexton *together* had killed her brother? That Brexton might've then wanted her dead to clear himself? No, it didn't add up; the police weren't that stupid. They knew something I didn't or they were bluffing.

Alma Edderdale invited us all to her cabana. Liz and I followed her, leaving Elmer to circulate importantly among the important members of the Club.

Lady Edderdale's cabana was a choice one on the end of the row, with a bright awning, a porch and a portable bar. A half dozen of us arranged ourselves in deck chairs. The afternoon was splendid with that silver light you only get in the autumn by the sea.

Lady Edderdale talked to me for some minutes. At last she began to place me. She seemed almost interested when I told her I was staying with Mrs. Veering.

"Poor dear Rose," she murmured. "What a frightful thing to have happen! Brexton was my favorite modern old master too. Why should anyone want to have murdered him?"

I tried to explain that it was not Brexton but his wife who'd been murdered but Alma only nodded like a near-sighted horse confronted with oats in the middle-distance.

"His wife, Peggy, was always a trial, wasn't she? But, poor darling, what will she do without him now? She was Rose's daughter, you know."

I gave up. Lady Edderdale's confusion was legendary. She ambled on in her rather British, dying-fall voice. "Yes, it must be a strain for all of them. I'm sure the person who killed him must be *terribly* sorry now. I should be, shouldn't you? Such a fine painter, I mean. How *is* Rose, by the way? I haven't seen her yet."

I said she was as well as could be expected.

"Yes, I'm sure she's very brave about it all. It happened to me, you know. Right out of a clear sky too.

148

They came one day and said: Lady Edderdale, we'll want a new accounting. Of course I didn't know what they were talking about so I told them I *never* did accounts but my lawyer did. They went to him and, before you know it, I had to pay over a hundred thousand dollars."

I had the sensation of being caught in a nightmare. Either Lady Edderdale had gone completely off her rocker or I had or we both had. I looked desperately at Liz but she was sunning herself wantonly beside a thick white Swede.

"Hundred thousand dollars?" I repeated the one thing which I'd managed to salvage from her conversation.

"More or less. I don't know the exact sum but it was simply *awful* trying to get that much in such short time. They are relentless. I hope they give Rose a little more time than they gave me."

"Time?"

"Yes, to pay them."

"Them?"

"Those awful Income Tax people."

Then it was all clear. "How long ago did Rose find out she'd have to pay all that money?"

"Well, not too long ago. I'm awfully bad about time. We lunched at the Colony I remember with Chico Pazzetti ... you know Chico? His wife's left him by the way."

"She told you this at the Colony? Recently?"

"A month ago, yes. I remember she was in town for several days; she'd come down to talk to them, to the Bureau of Internal Revenue people, about the thing."

"Just what kind of ... thing was it?"

Alma sighed and waved her emerald-laden arms helplessly in the air. "I don't know, really. I know she was awfully upset and she wanted to talk to me because I'd gone through the same thing. I was no help, I fear. I think she said a hundred thousand ... or was that what *I* had to pay? No, we *both* had to pay that much and

on short notice. I remember saying we were in the
same boat except of course Rose, poor darling, really
hasn't much money any more."

4

I told Liz I'd call her later that day, if I got a
chance. Then, excusing myself, I went back to the
North Dunes.

The house looked peaceful and strangely empty, as
though no one lived there any longer. A prophecy? It
was nearly empty too, I found, when I went inside. Everyone was out for the day except Miss Lung who sat
at Mrs. Veering's desk with the proofs of the penulti-
mate "Book-Chat" in her hand.

"You see me at my labors," said the penwoman, re-
moving her glasses with a smile equally compounded of
lechery and silliness. Yet she was not really a fool; I
was beginning to see that.

"I went to see Allie," I said, sitting down in the
chair next to the desk, where I had had so many inter-
views with Greaves.

"Oh? I didn't know anybody was allowed to see her?"

"They let me in. She's much better."

"I'm glad. I'm devoted to Allie. By the way, I'm
doing Pearl Buck this week. I think her Indian phase
so fascinating ... especially after all the China she's
done. I mean, there's just so much China to do and
then one wants a change." She read me the entire
column of "Book-Chat." I applauded weakly.

"Hard at work?" Mrs. Veering, looking businesslike
and steady appeared in the alcove; she removed a sensible hat. "What a day! The first chance I've had to get
any work done."

Miss Lung got to her feet. "I was just having the
nicest chat with Mr. Sargeant. I was testing my column
on him: you know how I am about 'reader response.'
If only more writers would attempt, as I do, to gauge

150

exactly the average response and then strive to that goal, as I do. I believe in making a direct contact with the average mind on *every* level."

I excused myself, average mind and all.

I took a short walk on the beach in front of the house. The light was dimming; the silver day was becoming gold. I realized that no one had yet found the spot where Claypoole had been killed. It would probably be impossible to tell now: he had been dragged on the beach, probably close to the water so that the surf would hide the murderer's footprints. I had a hunch the murder had taken place close to the house, probably just out of sight, behind the dunes. Yet why wouldn't the murderer leave the body where it was? Why drag it to the terrace ... a risky business, considering the house full of police?

Something kept eluding me; it was like a word temporarily forgotten which the tongue almost remembers but the mind refuses to surrender up.

It was no use. Two gulls circled the sea. In the north the blue sky was smudged with gray: a storm approaching? The first blast of winter? I shivered and went into the house. I had one more errand to perform that day.

5

Brexton was seated gloomily on a bunk in the rather picturesque jail of Easthampton. He wore civilian clothes (I'd half-expected to see him in a striped suit) and he was sketching with a bit of charcoal on a pad of paper.

"Therapy," he said with a smile as I came in. "You don't look much like my lawyer."

"It was the only way I could get in. I told the police I was a junior partner of Oliver and Dale. You look pretty comfortable."

"I'm glad you think so. Sit down."

I sat down on a kitchen chair by the barred window. The branch of a green-foliaged tree waved against the window: I felt like a prisoner myself.

"I don't think you did it," I said.

"That makes two of us. What can I do for you?"

"Three. I talked to Allie this morning. I don't see how they could possibly arrest you in the light of her testimony."

"But they have." He put the pad down on the bed beside him and wiped charcoal smudges off his fingers with the edge of the blanket.

"I'm doing a piece about this for the *Globe*. I guess you've been following them."

He nodded, without any comment.

"Well, I'm trying to solve the case on my own and I think you know who murdered Claypoole. I think you might even have watched the murderer roll the body under the swing. Your window looked directly onto the terrace, onto the swing."

He chuckled softly. "If that's an example of your detective methods, I'm lost. For one thing I wasn't in my own room until a good deal later and, for another thing, I was still sleeping in the room on the ground floor."

"Oh," I looked at him stupidly. I had missed on that all right, missed cold. I began to feel a little shaky about my deductive powers. "Well, that rules that out." I rallied. "Where were you exactly at the time of Claypoole's death?"

"Sitting in the dark mostly, with Allie, on the porch."

"Did either of you leave the porch at that time, while the lights were out?"

"Yes, as a matter of fact both of us did, for short periods. I went to see the man on duty about the lights but I couldn't find him. I guess he was hunting for the fuse box. Then I came back and Allie and I talked for a while. She left the room to get a book she'd brought me but forgotten to give me, an art book. . . ."

"All this in the dark?"

152

"There was a lot of moonlight. You could see perfectly well. She got the book from her room. We talked for a bit and then went to bed. The rest you know."

"What did you talk about?"

"Mildred mostly."

"You didn't talk about the possibility of marriage, did you? I mean between you and Allie."

"That's nobody's business," said Brexton sharply.

"I'm sorry." I shifted ground. "What do you know about Mrs. Veering's tax problems?"

He gave me a slow, amused smile. "You know about that?"

"Not much ... just gossip. I gather she's being stuck for a great deal."

"Quite a bit." Brexton nodded. "Over a hundred thousand dollars."

"Can she pay it?"

"I suppose so, but it'll wreck her income."

"How does she happen to have to pay all that?"

"Well, the Veerings have a foundry out West. It does well enough and her interest in it pays her a large income. Her late husband's brother runs the business and looks after everything. Rose has got a good business head herself. She started out as a secretary to old man Veering, the president of the company. He married her, died and left her his share. Now it seems that recently the brother pulled some fast business deals ... mergers, that kind of thing. I'm not much on business ... I *do* know it had something to do with a capital gains tax which really wasn't, if you follow me. The government found out and now Rose and the brother both have to cough up a hundred thousand cash. . . ."

"And Mrs. Veering hasn't got it?"

"Not without selling most of her interest in the foundry."

"Then you'd say she was in a tough spot?"

"Yes, I'd say she was in a very tough spot." Brexton spoke slowly, his eyes on the green branch which softly scraped the bars of the window.

I played my hunch. "Was your wife a wealthy woman, Mr. Brexton?"

He knew what I was up to but he gave no sign; he only looked at me without expression. "Yes, she was."

"She was wealthy on her own . . . not through Mrs. Veering? Not through her aunt?"

"That's right. My wife's money came from the other side of her family."

"Did Mrs. Veering try to borrow money from your wife?"

Brexton stirred restlessly on the bunk; his hands clasped and unclasped. "Did Allie tell you this?"

"No, I'm just playing a long shot."

"Yes, Rose tried to get Mildred to help her out of this tax settlement. Mildred refused."

Neither of us said anything for a moment; then: "Why did your wife refuse?"

"I don't know. I suppose it was too much money, even for her. They had a terrible scene the night before she was drowned. I guess you heard the screams. Both had awful tempers. Mildred attacked Rose with my palette knife (by the way, I never saw it again after that night . . . until it was found beside Fletcher's body). I broke it up and calmed Mildred down."

"I should've thought it would have been the other way around: Mrs. Veering should have been the hysterical one, for having been turned down."

"They both were. They were a good deal alike, you know: mean-tempered, unbalanced. Mildred wanted to leave the house right then but I talked her out of it; by the next morning she was all right again."

"Do you think that was why your wife was invited . . . you were both invited for the week end . . . to help Mrs. Veering?"

Brexton nodded. "I know it. I think that's why Mildred got so angry. She knew Rose was getting tired of her behavior. Rose had dropped us flat for almost a year. Then, when this invitation came, Mildred was really kind of bucked up; she always regarded Rose as the social arbiter of the family and it hurt her when

Rose wouldn't see us any more. But then when she found out after dinner that first night that we'd only been asked down because Rose needed money, she blew up. I'm afraid I didn't altogether blame her."

"Do you think your wife, under ordinary circumstances, would have let her have the money?"

Brexton shrugged. "She might have. It was an awful lot though. But then I never did know how much money Mildred had. She always paid her bills and I paid mine. That was part of our marriage agreement."

"You had a written agreement?"

"No, just an understood one. Mildred was a good wife for me . . . strange as that may seem to anybody who only knew her during this last year."

I shifted to the legal aspects of the situation. "What line do you think the prosecution will take?"

"I'm not sure. Something wild, I think. My lawyers are pretty confident but then, considering what I'm paying them, they ought to be." He chuckled. "They should be able to buy all the evidence they need. But, seriously, they can't figure what Greaves has got on his mind. We thought Allie's testimony would convince even the District Attorney's office. Instead, they went right ahead and called the Special Court for Friday and stuck me in here."

"I suppose they're going chiefly on motive; you killed your wife because you didn't like her and wanted her money . . . maybe they'll prove you wanted to marry Allie which would explain why she gave you an alibi."

"Except why should I want to kill her brother? The one person she was really devoted to?"

"I think they'll just pick a motive out of the air . . . whatever fits . . . and use the presence of your knife beside the corpse as primary evidence."

"Thin," said Brexton, shaking his head.

"Fortunately, the prosecution doesn't know about the quarrel you had with Claypoole after your wife drowned. They probably know what we all know . . . that he cursed you when she died . . . but they don't

155

know about the fight you had in your room, the one I heard while sitting on the porch."

Brexton's self-control was admirable. He showed no surprise, only interest. "You heard that?"

"Most of it, yes. Claypoole blamed you for killing your wife. Not directly . . . at least I don't think that's how he meant it. I couldn't be sure. The impression I got was that he was holding you responsible, in some way, and that he was going to expose you."

"Well, that was about it." Brexton's tone could not have been more neutral, less informative.

"I haven't any intention of telling the District Attorney this."

"That's very nice of you."

"But I'd like to know what it meant . . . that conversation. What *you* meant when you said you'd tell everything too."

Brexton paused thoughtfully before answering; his quick, shrewd painter's eyes studying me as though I were a model whose quality he was trying to fix exactly with a line. Then he said: "There's not much to tell. Mildred hounded Fletcher for the last few years, trying to get him to marry her. He wasn't interested though he'd been in love with her before she married me. Then, during the last year, he began to change. I think I know why. He started to see her. They took a trip to Bermuda together under assumed names. I found out . . . people always do. I gave Mildred hell, just on general principles. She promptly had a nervous breakdown; afterwards, she asked me for a divorce and I said not yet. I guess that was a mistake on my part. I wasn't in love with Mildred but I liked her and I was used to her and I suspected Claypoole was interested in her only on account of her money. Allie had told me how their income had begun to shrink these last few years, like everybody's else's. I think Fletcher decided the time had come to get himself a rich wife. He was furious with me for standing in his way. Then, when Mildred drowned, he was positive I had something to do with it, to keep her money for myself, to keep her from marrying him. That's all there was to it. He blew up and threatened to accuse me of murder . . . I have a hunch he did, before he died, and I think that's what Greaves is counting on to get me indicted. . . . Fletcher's accusation of me before he himself was murdered."

Now it was making sense. "One other thing: what did you mean when you told him you'd drag Allie into the case if he accused you?"

Brexton actually blushed. "Did I say that? I must've been near the breaking point. I'd never have done a thing like that. . . . I was just threatening, trying to warn him off."

"In what way could she have been brought into the case?"

"She couldn't, ever; what I said had to do . . . well, with other things, with her and me and her brother. I was only threatening: it was the worst thing I could think to say to him. Funny, I'd even forgotten I'd said it, until you mentioned it."

I was now fairly sure of the line the District Attorney would take. This was a help.

Then the jailer appeared, a fat policeman who waggled some keys and told me my time was up.

"Good luck," I said as we parted.

Brexton chuckled. "I'll need it." He picked up his sketch pad again. "I think you're moving in the right direction, Mr. Sargeant." But the policeman had me out of the cell block before I could ask him what he meant.

It was sundown when I got back to the house and parked Randan's car in the drive. It was pleasant not to be observed by policemen. They were all gone. Only Miss Lung, Mrs. Veering, Randan and myself were in the house, not counting servants.

I found Randan alone in the drawing room, writing furiously in a notebook, a highball beside him.

"Oh, hello." He looked up briefly to make sure I wasn't all broken up from an automobile accident. "Car all right?"

"Car's fine . . . ran over a small child but you'll be

157

able to square it with the parents: they seemed a broad-minded, modern couple." I fixed myself a martini.

"I'm writing up the case," said Randan, dotting a period firmly and shutting the notebook. "Going to do a serious piece on it."

I changed the subject. "Where are the beautiful ladies?"

"Making themselves more beautiful. Dinner's early tonight, in half an hour. Oh, your friend Liz called and asked me to ask you to join her at the party they're giving Alma Edderdale in Southampton tonight. I said I'd drive you down. . . ."

"And got yourself invited too?"

Randan looked pained by my bad taste. "I was only trying to be helpful."

"I'm sure of that. By the way, I saw Brexton this afternoon."

"In jail? I didn't know they'd let anybody in."

"I have influence. Did you try to see him too?"

Randan nodded. "Yes, I wanted to check on something. I'm beginning to get a little doubtful about the case," he added importantly.

"Doubtful? I thought you agreed with Greaves that Brexton . . ."

"I'm not so sure now. I . . . well, I overheard something this afternoon, here in the house. I don't like to appear to be an eavesdropper but . . ."

"But you listened to a conversation not meant for your ears. Perfectly common human trait . . . after all, what is history but a form of eavesdropping?" Fortunately, this was a rhetorical question. Randan ignored it.

"I heard Mrs. Veering talking to a lawyer."

"To Brexton's lawyer?"

"Yes . . . but they weren't talking about the murders. They were talking about a will, about Mrs. Brexton's will. It seems she left half her estate to her aunt, to Mrs. Veering. The other half she left to Claypoole. Her husband didn't get anything. Seems he even agreed to the will beforehand. Now what I was wondering . . ."

Chapter Eight

1

Dinner was a forced affair. Luckily, Miss Lung was in an ebullient mood and kept us in stitches with her "Book-Chat." I tried not to look at Mrs. Veering who had decided to have just a touch of Dubonnet against doctor's orders. She was so well lit by the time coffee was served that Randan and I were able to slip away without much explanation to anyone, except Miss Lung who was roguish.

It took almost half an hour to get from Easthampton to Southampton.

The moon was down and the night sky was partly obscured by clouds moving in from the north.

We didn't talk much, both occupied with our thoughts. At one point Randan tried to pump me about the tax case but I wasn't giving him any of my cherished leads. This was one story I intended to have all to myself.

It was just as we were getting out of the car in front of the mansion on Gin Lane where the party was being held, that Randan said: "I guess we both knew who did it."

I nodded. "We should've figured it out sooner. There were enough loose ends left flapping."

"I thought it was skillfully done." He switched off the ignition. "When did you catch on?"

"With Alma Edderdale yesterday. She let the cat out of the bag, talking about Rose's tax problems."

Randan nodded. "It ties in. You going to tell Greaves? Before the Special Court?"

I shook my head. "No, I'll try and work it out for the *Globe* first. Then, when I think I've got it plotted just right, I'll talk to Greaves ... that way I'll be sure to have the story before anybody."

We went to the party. I was feeling just fine, walking on clouds of fatuity.

The ballroom (it was, so help me, a ballroom) was a vast affair with parquet floors and huge pots of ferns and three chandeliers and a gallery where musicians played soft music. Everybody, as they say, was there.

I paid my respects to Lady Edderdale who stood with a bewildered expression beside her host, a man who had made his millions mysteriously in World War II ... no doubt stealing tires and selling them to the black market.

"Ah, yes, Mr. ...." she sighed as we shook hands, my name forgotten. "I have such an awful time with names but I never forget a face. When did you leave London?"

I got away as soon as I could and went through the milling throng to a dining room where a buffet, complete with four chefs, had been prepared and here, as I expected, was my light of love, gorging herself on smoked turkey and surrounded by a circle of plump, bald, dimpled bachelors.

"Peter! You could make it."

"With you any time," I said in my best vulgar Marlon Brando voice. The bachelors looked at me nervously; a stud trotting through a circle of horses to the nearest mare.

The mare looked particularly radiant in white and gold, wearing family diamonds which made me wonder if perhaps a marital alliance might be in order.

I glared at the bachelors and they evaporated. We were left with smoked turkey and champagne and Cole Porter from the orchestra in the ballroom and no one but people to interrupt our bliss.

"Why did you go running off like that this afternoon?" Liz looked at me curiously; I prayed for a jealous scene. But there was none. In fact, she didn't even wait for an excuse.

"I hear it's all over. Somebody told me Brexton won't have a chance, that they got a full confession."

"Are you sure?" This would be, as they said, the ultimate straw.

"No, I'm not really. It's just the rumor going around."

"What're you doing after this, hon?" I spoke out of the side of my mouth; the other side was full of food.

"Tonight? Well, I'm going home as every proper girl should."

"Let's go to bed."

"Bed?" she said this in such a loud startled voice that one of the chefs noticeably paled. "Bed?" she repeated in a lower voice. "I thought you only liked to romp among the cactuses ... or maybe you mean a bed of nails somewhere. . . ."

"Young women should never attempt irony," I said coldly. "It's not my fault that, through bad management, you haven't been able to provide me with the wherewithal to make love properly, preferably in a gilded cage. You have an income, don't you?"

"I want to be loved only for my money," she said, nodding agreeably. "After all beauty passes. Characters grow mean. But money, properly invested, is always lovable."

"Yours *is* properly invested? In gilt-edged or at least deckle-edged securities?"

"Yes, but I didn't know you cared."

"So much so that I am willing to put you up for the

night at the New Arcadia Motel, a center of illicit sexuality only a few miles from here."

"What will my family say?"

"That you are wanton. The money's in your name, isn't it?"

"Oh yes, Mummy had her second husband make me a trust fund . . . sweet, wasn't it?"

"Depends entirely on the amount." I started to put my arm stealthily around her when Elmer Bush came roaring down upon us.

"How's the boy? . . . say now! Is this the same pretty little girl I met today on the beach, Miss Liz Bessemer?"

"The same pretty little girl," agreed Liz with a dazzling smile. "And this, I suppose, is still the famed Elmer Bush who, through the courtesy of Wheat-mushlets, is heard over N.B.C. once a week?"

That slowed him up. "Quite a bright little girl, isn't she, Pete? You're some picker, boy. Well, I guess lucky in love unlucky in crime. Ha! Ha!" While we were doubled up with merry laughter at this sally, Liz stole quietly away.

"Say, didn't mean to barge in on you and the girl friend." Elmer positively smacked his lips as he followed Liz with his eyes as she strolled into the ballroom: all eyes were upon her, her shoulders bare and smooth above the white and gold dress.

"No, Elmer, I'd rather see you any day."

"Some kidder." Elmer was perfunctory now that there was no one around to impress except me and he knew of course I wasn't one of his fans. "Want you to do me a favor."

"What's that?"

"I'd like to get an interview with Mrs. Veering. I can't get through to her. She's playing hard to get. . . . God knows why since she's a real publicity hound. Now if you would . . ."

"But Elmer, we're rivals." I pretended surprise. "After all I'm still trying to get myself out of a hole. . . ."

"This is for the *Globe*. Not for me." He stood there,

noble, self-sacrificing. .... I half expected to hear the soft strains of the *Marseillaise* in the background.

"Well, I'm sorry, Elmer, but you'll have to get her on your own."

"Now look here, Sargeant, I've been sent here by the *Globe,* same paper that's been paying you for those dumb articles on why Brexton didn't do the murder. I can tell you one thing: you don't stand any too well around the office. Now if I tell them you've been cooperative, really helpful, they might not write you off as a complete loss." He stared at me, hard and menacing, the way he does when he attacks the enemies of a certain senator who is trying to root out corruption and Communists.

"Elmer," I said quietly, "I hate you. I have always hated you. I will always continue to hate you. There is nothing I would not do to show you the extent and beauty of my hatred. I would throw you a rock if you were drowning. I would . . ."

"Always the kidder," said Elmer with a mechanical smile to show that he knew I was joking. "Well, I'm not kidding. The paper expects you to cooperate. If you don't you might just as well give up all ideas of working for them again."

"Suppose I'm right?" I was getting tired of him fast but I realized my situation was hopeless anyway if I didn't produce the real story, and soon. He was out to cut my throat, as they say in the profession.

"That Brexton didn't kill his wife and Claypoole?" Elmer looked at me pityingly.

"I wouldn't bank too much on Claypoole's accusation, before he died." My shot in the dark hit the target.

Elmer blinked. "Know about that, eh?"

"That's right. I also know the prosecution is going to build its case on Claypoole having said Brexton murdered his wife. . . ."

"He told the whole story to the police the day he was murdered." Elmer looked smug, just as though he had done it all himself with his little hatchet. I was glad to hear my guess confirmed. Elmer had served his purpose.

2

"I'm sure they'll check up on me, just to be unpleasant." Liz sat with nothing on in front of the dressing table, arranging her hair: she is one of those women who do their hair and face before dressing. I lay on the bed, blissful, enjoying the morning sun which fell in a bar of light across my belly. It had been an excellent night . . . morning too. Nothing disturbed me.

"What do you care?" I said, yawning.

"I don't really." I watched her shoulder blades as she made mysterious passes at her hair and face, her back to me. "It's just that when I said I was staying with friends in Southampton I shouldn't've mentioned Anna Trees. They're bound to see her and my aunt will ask her about my overnight stay and . . ."

"And you're worrying too much. Besides, I'm sure your aunt would approve of the New Arcadia. Clean sheets. Private bathroom. View of a roadhouse and U.S. Route One as well as the company of a red-blooded American boy. . . . Come here."

"Not a chance in the world, Peter." She rose with dignity and slipped on her silk pants. "You've had your kicks, as they say . . . brutish, prancing goat. . . ."

"I never prance." I wanted her again but she had other plans. Sadly, I got up myself and went into the bathroom to take a shower. When I came out, Liz was fully dressed and going through the wastebasket in the preoccupied way women have when they are minding someone else's business.

"Ah, ah," I said sharply, the way you do to a child. "Might find something dirty. Don't touch."

"Nonsense." Liz pulled out a newspaper and a cigarette butt. "Just as I thought: marijuana. I thought I smelled something peculiar."

"Well, don't touch it. I thought all women were mortally afraid of germs."

"Stop generalizing." Liz dropped the butt back into the wastebasket and opened the newspaper absently. I got dressed.

A sharp sound from Liz halted me. "Is *this* Claypoole?" she asked, holding the paper for me to see.

I took it from her. It was a Monday edition of The *Journal American.* There were several photographs of the principals involved in our local killing. One was of Claypoole. I nodded, giving her the paper back; I combed my hair in the dusty mirror. "What about it?"

"Well, I know him."

"Knew him. So what? A lot of people did."

"No, but I saw him only recently. I didn't really know him but I think I met him . . . or ran into him, or something." She paused, confused, poring over the newspaper intently. "I know!" She squealed.

"Well?"

"It was Sunday night, at the Club . . . before I went on to Evan Evans' party. I dropped in with some people, with a boy I know. We looked around just to see who was there. It was dead, you know the way Sunday night is, so I had my escort drive me over to Evan's . . . anyway, before I left I remember seeing him, Claypoole, ever so distinctly. He was awfully good-looking in an older way; I noticed him because he was by himself, in a plain suit. Everybody else was dressed. He was standing all alone in the door which opens onto the terrace. . . ."

"You didn't speak to him?"

"No, I just caught the one glimpse."

"What time was it?"

"Time? Well, not much after twelve thirty."

I was excited. "You realize that you may be the last person to've seen him alive?"

"Really?" She was properly impressed. "I don't suppose it proves anything, does it? He must've strolled over from the North Dunes. Peter, I'm starved, let's get some breakfast."

Stealthily, we left the New Arcadia Motel, the way hundreds of couples every week did, their unions blessed only by the gods of love, the sterner bonds of society momentarily severed or ignored.

We found a pleasant inn just south of the village of Easthampton where we ate a huge breakfast. It was an odd morning with a white mist high overhead through which the sun shone diffused, bright but not concentrated.

"I love those spur-of-the-moment adventures," said Liz, eating more eggs than I've ever seen a slender girl eat before.

"I hope you don't have a great many of them."

"As many as I can squeeze in without being untidy," she said comfortably, leaving me to guess whether she was serious or not.

"I suppose next thing, you'll tell me you do this all the time, in motels."

"There's an awfully disagreeable streak of Puritanism in you, Peter. I worry about it."

"I just want to be able to think of you as being all mine, clean from the word go."

"From the word go, yes." Liz beamed at me over coffee. She was a beautiful creature, more like an act of nature than a human being ... I thought of her in elemental terms, like the wind or the sky, to wax lyrical. Usual laws of morality didn't apply to her.

I changed the subject ... just looking at her upset me. "How much longer do you intend to stay down here?"

Liz sighed. "Tomorrow I go back. I tried to talk them into letting me stay longer but they wouldn't. I don't think any magazine should try to put out issues in the hot weather. Nobody'll read them."

"Who reads fashion magazines? Women just buy them to look at the pictures of clothes."

"Well, it's an awful strain working in New York in

166

the hot weather. I was supposed to go back yesterday but I got an extra day. When will you be back?"

"Friday. I'll have to stay here for the Special Court, to testify. I'll go back to New York right afterwards."

"What an interesting week end it turned out to be," said Liz, putting ice from her drinking glass into her coffee cup. "I don't know why I never ask for iced coffee when I hate it hot. Peter, do you really think Brexton's innocent?"

I nodded.

"But if he didn't do it, who did?"

"Somebody else."

"Oh, don't be silly! Who could possibly have done it?"

"Somebody with a motive."

"Well, you must have some idea who it was if you're so certain it wasn't Brexton."

"Oh, I know who did it all right." And I did. I had known for nearly half an hour.

Liz's eyes grew round. "You mean you're sitting right here having breakfast with me like this and you know who killed Mrs. Brexton and Claypoole?"

"I can't see what having breakfast with you has to do with it but, yes, I know who the murderer is. Thanks to you."

"To me? What have I done?"

"I'll tell you later."

Liz looked at me as though she wasn't sure whether or not to telephone for a squad of men in white. She tried the practical approach. "What're you going to do about it now that you think you know everything?"

"Now that I know, not think. I'm sure. I have to tie up some ends first. Even then I may not be able to prove what I know."

"Oh, Peter, tell me! Who is it?"

"Not on your life." I paid for breakfast and stood up. "Come on, dear. I've got to take you home."

"I have never in my life known such a sadist." Liz was furious and persistent but I wouldn't tell her anything. She hardly spoke to me when we pulled up in front of the North Dunes and I got out. She slid haughtily into the driver's seat. "It's been very nice, Mr. Sargeant."

"I've had a swell time too."

"Beast!" And Liz wheeled out of the driveway on two wheels, the gears screeching with agony. Smiling to myself, I went into the house. I had a tough day ahead of me.

3

No one but the butler was in sight when I arrived. He bade me good morning and made no comment about my night out. I went upstairs to my bedroom and immediately telephoned Miss Flynn.

"I have undertaken the Tasks assigned," she said, in her stately way. "The following are the Results of my Herculean Labors." She gave me several pieces of information; one was supremely useful. I told her to expect me Friday afternoon and, after a bit of business, we rang off.

I was surprisingly calm. The identity of the killer had come to me that morning with Liz. Something she said had acted like a catalyst: everything fell into place at once ... all those bits of disconnected information and supposition had, with one phrase, been fused into a whole and I knew with certainty what had happened, and why.

I packed my suitcase; then I went downstairs and left it in the hall. I was not going to spend another night in this house.

On the terrace, watching the mist grow dense, become fog, was Miss Lung. She was sitting quite alone with a brilliant Guatemala shawl about her shoulders.

She jumped when I approached. "Oh, Mr. Sargeant. What a start you gave me! A little bird told me you didn't come home last night."

"The little bird was on the beam," I said, sitting down beside her. "Looks like a storm coming up."

She nodded. We both looked out to sea, or rather at the line of gun-metal gray breakers: the horizon was gone already and fog was rolling in from the sea in billows. It was suddenly chilly, and uncomfortably damp.

"We have had such lovely weather," said Miss Lung nostalgically. "I suppose this must be the end of summer. It comes like this, doesn't it, all at once."

"Not until later, about the time of the equinox," I said absently, watching her out of the corner of my eye. She was unusually pale, her book-chat manner entirely discarded. I could almost imagine the slender good-looking woman imprisoned beneath the layers of fat and disappointment. "You were very fond of Mr. Claypoole, weren't you?"

"What makes you ask?" She looked at me, startled.

"I'm curious about this case, that's all. I've always thought there were some very important facts the police didn't know."

"I'm sure there's a great deal of importance the police don't know," said Miss Lung sharply. "And I'm in favor of keeping them ignorant, aren't you?"

"In general, yes. That was what you meant, though, wasn't it? About not wanting too close an investigation . . . you remember the other day when you told me. . . ."

"Yes, I remember. I have nothing criminal to hide. It's certainly no secret about Fletcher and me. I'm sure if it hadn't been for Allie (whom I adore, believe me) we might have married once. She wouldn't let him; then Mildred tried, and failed too . . . that's all."

"Yet why should that bother you? I mean what difference would it make if it should all come to light, about you and Fletcher?"

Miss Lung paused before answering; then she said, with an odd look in her eyes, "I'll tell you exactly what I feared, Mr. Sargeant, but you must promise me never to refer to this to anyone, certainly never to write about it in the press. Do you promise?"

"Well . . . yes, I promise."

"I was afraid that if the police should start prying around in our past, Fletcher's, Paul's, mine, they would sooner or later discover that Paul Brexton painted me, fifteen years ago, in the . . . well the altogether. You must know that I have fans everywhere in the United States and Canada and if that painting should ever come to light and be reproduced in the Yellow Press I would be absolutely finished as the authoress of 'Book-Chat.' You see now my fear of investigation?"

It was all I could do to keep from laughing. "I see exactly what it is you feared. As a matter of fact, I did hear about the painting."

"You see? Already people have begun to talk about it! Ever since this hideous business started I've been in mortal dread of someone unearthing that picture. In my last conversation with Paul before he was taken to jail, I implored him to keep silent on that subject, come what may."

"I'm sure he will. I hear, by the way, it was quite a good painting."

"I was not ever thus," said Miss Lung, with a brief return of her sly-boots self.

We chatted a while longer. Then I went into the house. Everything was shaping up nicely. So nicely that I was scared to death.

On the second floor, I slipped into Brexton's room. No one saw me. The room had been straightened and now looked perfectly ordinary. I checked the lock of the door to what had been Allie's room (another key replaced the one the prosecution had taken for an exhibit); the lock worked smoothly. Then I went to the window and examined the screen. As I expected, there were scratches on the sill, at either corner. Long regular scars in the weathered wood. Tentatively, I pressed my finger against the screen: it was loose. I was not able to check the other windows for, as I was about to enter Allie's room, Mrs. Veering appeared in the doorway.

"Mr. Sargeant!" She seemed genuinely surprised. "What are you doing in there?"

"I ... I was just looking for something," I stammered stupidly.

"In *this* room? I can't think what," she said flatly, as though suspecting me of designs on the flat silver. "Mary Western told me you were back. I'd like to talk to you."

"Certainly." We went downstairs to her alcove off the drawing room.

She was all business, a tumbler of Dubonnet on the desk in front of her. "I've decided to go ahead with the party," she said.

I was surprised. "I thought . . ."

"At first, I thought it would be in bad taste. Now I think I can't afford to back out of it. People expect one to carry on." She took a long swallow of Dubonnet, carrying on.

"You may be right," I said. "I'm afraid though I won't be able to handle it. I'm due in New York Friday. . . ."

"Oh. Well, I'm sorry. If it's a matter of fee. . . ." She seemed disturbed by my refusal.

"No, it's not that at all. I just have an awful lot of work piling up and . . ." I made a series of glib and, I hoped, plausible excuses. I couldn't tell her my real reason; she would find out soon enough.

"I'm very sorry. I hope at least you'll still be kind enough to advise me now."

I said that I would and we had a brisk business talk in which I confided to her what I'd felt all along: that she was quite capable of mapping out a publicity campaign on her own. She took this without elation or demur.

"Thank you. I do my best. As you probably know, I have had certain difficulties lately." She looked at me shrewdly to see how I'd react; I didn't bat an eye; I looked at her as though it was the first I'd heard of these troubles.

She continued, satisfied apparently with my silence.

171

"People have actually started a rumor that I've been wiped out financially. Well, it isn't true and for that reason I don't dare *not* give this party. I sent the invitations out this morning."

So that was it. She was spending Mildred's money before she got it. I couldn't blame her under the circumstances . . . it was an act of God.

4

To my surprise Allie Claypoole and Greaves showed up together for lunch.

She was pale and she walked as though she were unsure of her legs, like an invalid new-risen. Greaves was jubilant in a restrained, official way.

"Certainly is nice to see everybody like this," he said. "Not official or anything like that."

"We're always happy to see *you,* Mr. Greaves," said Mrs. Veering smoothly from the head of the table. The butler passed champagne around. It was quite a luncheon.

Randan and Allie sat next to each other and talked in low voices through most of the lunch while the rest of us either listened to Mary Western Lung or drank our champagne in silence.

It wasn't until dessert that I was able to turn to Greaves who was on my left and ask a question which could not be heard by the rest of the table: Miss Lung was loudly recounting a bit of scandal which had taken place at a meeting of the Ladies' Paintbox and Typewriter Club.

"What did the knife look like?" I asked in a low voice.

Greaves looked surprised. "Knife?"

"Yes, the one they found beside Claypoole. I never got a close look at it."

"Just an ordinary knife, very sharp. A kind of

172

kitchen knife with a bone handle and Brexton's initials on it."

"Initials?" That was it! "Were they prominent?"

"Yes, they were pretty big. What're you up to, Sargeant?" He looked at me suspiciously.

"I may have a surprise for you."

"Like what?"

"Like the real killer."

Greaves snorted. "We got him and don't you go rocking the boat. We have enough trouble without your interference. Elmer Bush's told me about the way you operate. I told him if you tried anything . . ."

"Elmer is my best friend," I said, hardly able to contain my delight. "One other question and then I'm through. Sunday morning Claypoole said he went to the John Drew Theater to look at the paintings. Well, I happen to know the theater was closed that morning, I figure he went to see you."

"What if he did?" Greaves squirmed uncomfortably.

"I have a hunch he drove over to Riverhead and told you Brexton murdered his wife. I believe your District Attorney, misled by you, is building his case and political ruin on that visit."

"I don't like your tone, Sargeant." Greaves had turned very red. "But since you know so much already I'll tell you that, yes, Claypoole came to see me and he accused Brexton. I don't think Brexton knew it . . . that's why he killed him that same night, to keep him quiet, not knowing it was already too late. I should've acted right away. I realize that now but I didn't think anything could happen in a house with two M.C.I. men on hand. Anyway it's all over. Nobody can save your friend Brexton," said Greaves, quietly folding his napkin and placing it beside his plate.

"He's not my friend; he's also not your clay pigeon, Greaves."

"Now look here. . . ." but Mrs. Veering had got to her feet; she led us all into the drawing room for coffee.

I got Allie Claypoole away from Randan for a moment. "You're not giving in, are you?"

173

"About Paul?" She sighed and sat down shakily. I sat down beside her. "I don't know what to think. Greaves has been with me all morning. He's trying to make me believe Paul tried to murder me but I can't . . . I just *won't* believe it."

"Good," I said. "You stick by what you feel. You're right."

She clenched her slender white hands into two fists. "But if Paul didn't who *could've* done it?"

"The same person who killed your brother."

"Do you know who it is?"

I nodded. She looked at me with real terror in her eyes. Then Greaves, suspecting I might be intimidating a valuable witness, joined us and I excused myself.

I was about to go telephone 1770 House to see if they might have a room for the night when Randan, with a smirk, said: "What happened to you and Liz? Suddenly you both just disappeared and Miss Lung tells me you didn't come home at all last night. I looked around for you when I left but you'd gone by then."

"Miss Bessemer and I spent the night with the *Times* crossword puzzle at the New Arcadia Motel," I said and walked away.

I made a reservation for that night by telephone. Then I slipped out of the house by way of the front door. I wanted one more look around before I finished my case.

I walked among the umbrellas on the terrace, sad-looking in the gray fog which had already blotted out the ocean only a few yards away. It was as thick a fog as I'd ever seen. The umbrellas looked like monsters, looming in the mist.

Then I took out my watch and began to walk, at a good pace, down the beach to the Club.

Five minutes later I reached the Club.

It was a strange walk. I couldn't see more than a few feet in front of me. If it hadn't been for a cluster of rotten black pilings which marked the beginning of the Club beach I shouldn't have known where I was. The

174

Club House was invisible. There was no sound from its general direction.

I had the impression of being packed in cotton wool. I almost felt that if I put my hand out I could touch the fog, a gray heavy damp substance.

Far out to sea, I heard the horn of a ship, lonely and plaintive. Well, it would soon be over, I told myself. I was oddly depressed. I had solved the case but there was no elation, only relief and perhaps a certain fear.

I made my way back slowly. I followed the edge of the water which eddied back upon the white sand. If I hadn't, I would've got lost for there were no landmarks: nothing but white sand and gray fog.

I timed my return trip so that I'd know when I was abreast the North Dunes. Otherwise I knew I might keep on until Montauk without ever knowing where I was.

I was three minutes and two seconds from the Club when a figure appeared, tall and dark. We both stopped at the water's edge: each had been following the water line. Then Randan approached. He was carrying my suitcase.

"I thought you were taking a walk," he said amiably. "I followed you."

"You thought I'd walk to the Club?"

He nodded. "It's a nice walk, isn't it? Perfect for a foggy day."

"I like the fog." I glanced at the suitcase in his hand: this was it at last. I knew what was coming. "Not such a good walk, though, if you're carrying something."

"Like your suitcase?" he grinned.

"Or like your uncle."

The smile faded from his face. We were only a yard apart and yet his features were faintly blurred by the intervening fog, white and enveloping. We stood within a circle of visibility whose diameter was not more than a yard. Somewhere far above, in another world, the afternoon sun was shining. We were like the last survivors of a disaster, alone with our secrets.

A wave broke close to us. Water swirled about our

shoes. Simultaneously we moved farther up the shore, each keeping the other in range. Was he armed? The question repeated itself over and over in my brain. If he was. . . .

"You know a great deal," said Randan. He put the suitcase down. He was wearing a trench coat, I noticed . . . very sensible, I thought inanely, keep the damp out: fog caressed us like damp cotton; my clothes were soaked, and not only from fog.

"I have my suspicions," I said, trying to sound casual. "But they don't do me much good since there's no evidence of any kind." Anything to throw him off the track. I was positive he was armed. I planned a sudden break up the beach, into the fog. One leap and I'd be out of sight. But if he were armed. . . .

"You're not stupid," Randan sounded somewhat surprised.

"Thanks. Unfortunately neither are you. There's no way of making a case against you. I think I know exactly what happened but there's no proof of any kind. You thought of everything." But he was too smart for such flattery. I was talking fast, to no point. My suitcase in his hand meant this was the pay-off.

"Tell me what you know, Sargeant." The question was put quietly, without emphasis.

"Not enough."

"Tell me anyway." He put his hand in the pocket of his coat. I went death-cold: was he armed? Was he armed?

I decided to talk, my legs tensed for a spring into the whiteness about us, into the protecting, the murderous fog. My mouth was dry. Sweat trickled down my side. With difficulty I kept my voice steady. "I think you made your plan in Boston, the night before you came here. You heard about the murder on the radio . . . or rather the mysterious death of Mildred Brexton. You knew her husband would be held responsible. You also knew of Fletcher's dislike of Brexton, on Mildred's account. On a wild chance, you thought there might be

176

an opportunity for you to kill your uncle, making it look as though Brexton had killed him."

"All this from having heard over the radio that Mildred Brexton drowned accidentally?" He sounded amused.

I nodded. "Also from a conversation with Allie, by telephone, the day before. I think she told you pretty much the situation down here. You knew what to expect." This was a guess. It was accurate.

"I didn't think Allie would mention that telephone call," said Randan. "Yes, that gave me the ... the background of the week-end party. Go on."

"Just in case, you prepared, in Boston, the note saying Brexton was the killer. I had my secretary check the Boston papers for your last day there: none carried an account of Mildred's death ... too soon. Because of that you weren't able to get an X or a K out of the headlines. This bothered me when I first saw the note. I figured that anyone of us preparing such a note would have had no trouble finding Xs and Ks since the papers were full of references to Brexton, to Mildred's death."

"Good, very good." Randan seemed pleased. "I was worried that the police might discover my note was made from Boston papers. Fortunately, they were so positive Fletcher fixed the note that they didn't bother tracking it down. Then what happened?"

"You arrived in the early morning, Sunday, by car. You went straight to the house. The guard was asleep. You looked around. In the living room you found Brexton's palette knife with his initials on it, left there after Mildred attacked Mrs. Veering Friday night. You took it, for future use. You were in the kitchen ... perhaps examining the fuse box, when I arrived. You struck me with. . . ."

"Of all homely items, a rolling pin." Randan chuckled. "Not hard enough either." A gull shrieked. The surf whispered.

"You then left the house, making your official appearance later on that day. You found out soon enough what was going on. Your uncle no doubt told you he

177

suspected Brexton of murdering his wife. He might even have told you of his denunciation of Brexton to the police. If he did, and I think he did, the moment was right. Your uncle had accused Brexton of murder. Your uncle is murdered. Brexton, without a doubt, would be held responsible. The rest was comparatively simple."

"I'm all ears."

I watched his face while I talked, reading his responses in his expression rather than his words. I recapitulated quickly. "Mildred died by accident. Brexton knew this. The rest of us did too until that policeman, prodded by your vindictive uncle, scenting an easy case, decided to make something out of it. Both he and your uncle played your game to perfection ... to their regret."

"Greaves will certainly benefit. He's already a hero." Randan was smug. I played right along.

"That's right. I don't suppose Greaves will ever know that he's sent an innocent man to the chair."

"No, he'll never know," Randan agreed cheerfully. "There'll be no one to tell him he was wrong."

I pretended not to get this but I did and I was ready: he was armed all right. Under cover of the fog he would commit his last murder, destroy the only witness of his cunning. I made plans while we talked.

"You fixed two alibis for Sunday night, the night you killed your uncle. First was at the Club. The second was at the Evans party where you ran into us ... an unexpected meeting, I'd say. You made a date to meet your uncle at the club around twelve thirty. You drove over. He walked ... along the beach. You met on the beach, I think, probably near the cabanas, in the dark. You talked. Perhaps you strolled away from the Club, toward the house. At some point you both sat down. You struck him on the head with some object. . . ."

"Very like a stone."

"And dragged him to the house where you knew the police would be busy with the tampered fuse box and

178

the others would've gone to bed. You then cut Claypoole's throat with Brexton's knife and rolled the body under the swing, leaving the knife near by to implicate Brexton. Aware that friend Greaves would be sufficiently simple to think that a man of Brexton's intelligence would leave a knife with his own prints and initals on it beside a dead body."

"Pretty good, Sargeant. You've missed a few subtle touches here and there but you have the main points. Go on."

"Then you went back to the Club, putting in a second appearance, pretending you were there all along. After that you went on to Evans' party. You didn't make a single mistake." I laid it on. I had two alternatives. One was to disappear into the fog and run the risk of being shot; the other was to try a flying tackle before he could pull the trigger of that pistol which, I was sure, was pointed at me in his trench-coat pocket.

While I made up my mind, I talked quickly . . . flattered him, made it appear that I thought he was in the clear, that I was only an appreciative audience, not dangerous to him. He was too smart to fall for this but he enjoyed hearing me praise him. "After all," he said, "you're the only person I'll ever be able to talk to about this. Tell me how you happened to suspect me. No one else did."

"Just luck. I told you something you didn't know, remember? I told you Allie had been with Brexton at the time of Claypoole's death. I knew this was something the murderer couldn't know and that the others hadn't heard. You acted quickly, as I thought you would. Allie must never regain consciousness. Her testimony would save Brexton. Her death would incriminate him once and for all. You had to kill her. At this point, though, you brought up a second line of defense which I admired particularly. Rose's tax difficulties. No doubt your uncle or Allie had told you about them. You knew she was a potential candidate for murderer of Mildred . . she had the best motives of all, really. You took one of her handkerchiefs with the idea of

179

planting it in Allie's room in case something went wrong. It would've implicated Rose but either you forgot to use it or else you were too sure of success. You came back to the house when the nurses were changed, at midnight. You had less than five minutes to give Allie the strychnine which you'd already got from Mrs. Veering's bathroom. You pushed the screen out of your window. You walked along the top of the porch to Allie's room. You pushed that screen in. You turned the key to Mrs. Veering's room which was lucky because you nearly had a visit from Miss Lung. You started to give Allie a hypodermic but there wasn't time to do it properly. Miss Lung had sounded an alarm. You unlocked the door between the two rooms, went back out the window to your own room and then made an appearance."

"Excellent." Randan was pleased to hear from me the story of his cleverness. "Couple of good details involved. One was planting the key to Allie's room in Brexton's pillow the day before ... just in case. The other was the business of the screens. Had to loosen them with a knife ... I thought I'd never get them right. Fortunately, they were all warped from the damp weather and they stuck in place even after being loosened. You're right about the handkerchief bit too. I was going to use it if Allie got Brexton off the hook."

"Your mentioning the murder of Sir Thomas Overbury helped put me on to you." I moved a millimeter closer to him. "The case was somewhat the same. . . ."

"Not at all the same. Did I mention him? I'd forgotten that. A slip. What else put you on to me?"

"A remark ... you said something about 'spur of the moment.' It stuck in my head; I don't know why. I never believed, frankly, that Mildred was murdered. Claypoole of course was. It could only have been a spur-of-the-moment murder, improvised on the spot, under cover of a suspected killing and arranged to fit in with the details of the first, the false murder. Then, last night, Liz gave me a piece of information I needed: she'd seen Claypoole at the Club a few minutes before

180

he died. Nobody knew he'd gone there. She got a glimpse of him only by chance. We knew that you had been there at the same time. Everything began to add up. Then, when I found out about the Boston newspapers. . . ."

"It's been nice talking to you." He stepped back a pace.

Soon. Soon. Soon. I braced myself. I talked fast. I inched toward him as I did. My plan decided up. "Why did you kill him though? That's one thing I could never figure out. I could never fix a proper motive."

"Money. He was permanent executor of my trust fund. As long as he lived I couldn't touch my own money until I was forty. I didn't want to wait until then. He was severe. I always hated him. When Mildred died I saw my chance. There'd never be another opportunity like it. I improvised, as you said. It was fascinating too. I've always studied murders. Planned them in my head, just for sport. I was surprised how easy it was to commit one . . . how easy to get away with it." I had moved, without his noticing it, a foot closer to him.

"But now," he said quietly, "Mr. Sargeant will unexpectedly leave Easthampton before the Special Court, baggage and all. By the time he is reported missing in Manhattan, Brexton will be well on his way. . . ."

I hit him low and hard. There was a pop, like a cork being blown from a bottle. A smell of gunpowder. For a moment, as we wrestled, I wondered if I'd been hit. Sometimes I knew, from the war, you could be shot and not know it.

But I was not hit. We fought hand to hand grimly at the water's edge. Randan swore and gasped and kicked and struggled like a weak but desperate animal; it was no use though and in a moment he lay flat on the sand, breathing hoarsely, barely conscious, a hole the size of a silver dollar burned in his coat where he'd fired at me . . . his revolver a yard away in the sand. I pocketed it. Then I picked him up and carried him back to the

house . . . sea foam, frothy as beer, in his hair . . . as I
followed the same route he himself had taken three days
before when he had dragged the unconscious body of
Fletcher Claypoole to the house.

5

"A Miss Bessemer is in the Outer Office," Miss
Flynn looked at me with granite eyes. "She has No Ap-
pointment."

"I'll see her anyway. Poor child . . . she was involved
in a white slave ring in Georgia. I'm trying to rehabili-
tate her."

Miss Flynn's reply was largely italics. She disappeared and Liz bounded into my office, her face glowing. "A hero! Darling Peter a hero! When I read about
it I didn't believe it was the same one I knew . . . the
same Peter Sargeant who. . . ." Words for once failed
her. I allowed her to kiss my cheek.

"I had no idea you were so brave. . . ."

"Ah."

"And so right." Liz sat down in the chair beside my
desk and stared at me.

I waved modestly. "I was merely doing my duty,
Ma'am. We here in southern Ontario feel that duty's
enough without any of this horn-blowing. . . ."

Liz's eyes narrowed thoughtfully. "I must say I suspected him too. Oh, I didn't say anything about it but I
had a hunch . . . you know how it is. Especially that
night at Evans' party, right after he killed his uncle . . .
his eyes were set too close together."

"Eyes?"

"You can always tell: eyes and hands . . . set too
close together means a criminal."

"His hands were set too close together. . . ."

"Now don't be maddening! He shot at you, didn't
he?"

I nodded calmly.

182

"Then you threw him to the ground and used judo to make him confess."

"A somewhat highly colored version of what happened," I said. "I was very brave though. Since he has the build of a somewhat frail praying mantis, you might say I had the edge on him."

"Even so he had a gun. I suppose he'll get the chair." She sounded matter-of-fact.

"Never can tell. They'll probably plead insanity ... especially after they read those notebooks of his. He gives the whole thing away ... writes about a perfect crime which resembles the one *he* committed. I think he was a kind of maniac. ..."

"Oh you could tell that just by looking at him. I knew the first time I ever laid eyes on him. Not that I ever thought he'd done it. ... I won't say that. ..."

"Yet."

"No, I won't say that but I *did* think him peculiar and you see how right I was. I've never seen so much space as the *Globe* gave you ... that Mr. Bush must've been livid."

"I think he was distressed." It made me feel good, thinking of Elmer's column being all chopped up because the issue which had contained my story had had a particularly well-displayed "America's New York" telling how Elmer himself had helped gather the evidence which was to send Brexton to his just reward.

"Where's Brexton now?"

"I don't know. I think he's gone off somewhere to hide ... also to marry Allie when this thing dies down." I got up and went over to a corner of the office where, face to the wall, was a large painting. "Brexton, with tears in his eyes, said he would give me anything I wanted: money, paintings ... anything. I asked for this." I turned the canvas around and there, triumphantly nude, reveling in her own golden skin was the young Mary Western Lung, not yet a penwoman, not yet the incomparable, fertile source of "Book-Chat."

183

Liz shrieked with pleasure. "It's Miss Lung! I can tell. You know she wasn't at all bad-looking."

"I intend to keep this in the office for all to see. I shall collect a small but useful sum each month to keep it out of the hands of her competitors and enemies. . . ."

"Her breasts were too big," said Liz critically, that sharp slanted mean look on her face that women assume when examining one another.

"Many people like them that way," I said, turning the picture back to the wall.

"Shall I go?"

"No, as a matter of fact there is an exercise which I've only just submitted to the patent office: it will make a pair of water wings out of the most non-descript. . . ." I was heading purposefully toward Liz when the little box on my desk spluttered, exactly like Miss Flynn. I answered it.

"That Mr. Wheen who has been trying to contact you . . . he is on the Wire." Miss Flynn's voice dripped acid . . . she knew what was going on in the Inner Office. "I'll talk to him," I said.

Liz came and sat on my lap, her hands were busy and embarrassing. "Stop that!" were the first words of mine Mr. Wheen heard.

"Stop what?" The voice was harsh, gravelly. "I just now got you, Mr. Sargeant. . . ."

"I didn't mean *you*, sir," I said smoothly. "I understand you've been trying to get in touch with me. . . ."

"Yeah, that's right. I think I got a job for you. It's about Muriel Sandoe."

"Muriel Sandoe? I don't think. . . ."

"She was an associate of mine. You know her maybe by her professional name in the circus: 'Peaches' Sandoe. Well, you see this elephant. . . ."